CALCULATED RISK

TRIUMPH OVER ADVERSITY

LYNN SHANNON

CALCULATED RISK

This novel is dedicated to the brave men and women of our military. Thank you for all that you do.

"But I will restore you to health and heal your wounds," declares the Lord

Jeremiah 30:17

ONE

Her cell phone rang.

Addison Foster glanced at the clock on her computer, concern rippling through her. It was close to midnight. Too late for a run-of-the-mill call. She scooped the cell from the desk in her home office. Chloe McCormick's name flashed on the screen. As a family law attorney for domestic abuse survivors, it wasn't uncommon for Addison to receive frightened phone calls from clients late at night. But they never got easier.

Addison answered. "Are you okay, Chloe?"

"I'm okay." Chloe's voice thickened with tears. "But I'm worried about going back to court on Tuesday, and you told me to call if I needed to."

The tremble of fear coursing through her client's voice was painful for Addison to hear. Chloe's husband, Michael McCormick, was a violent man protected by a fat bank account and influential friends. He'd beaten Chloe within an inch of her life over a dirty dish in the sink. Broken jaw, fractured ribs, and a concussion. The rules, so he thought, didn't apply to him. Everything about Michael put Addison on edge. Probably because he reminded her so much of her own ex-husband.

"You won't be alone for a moment with Michael during the divorce trial." Addison rubbed her eyes. She'd spent several hours staring at the computer, preparing for court by reviewing the McCormick's financial documents. "I'll be with you the entire time, just like today during the pre-trial motions."

"I know that. I'm just...I'm scared he'll try to do something before then. Michael always said he would kill me if I left." Her words tumbled out in a rush, layered with barely controlled panic. "I remembered what you told me. If he shows up, I need to call 911 immediately. But the police may not arrive in time. And Michael won't obey the restraining order. I know it. Did you see the way he looked at me in court today?"

Addison had. The rage had been tangible, and it hadn't only been directed toward his wife. Michael's glare had centered on Addison more than once. He blamed her for convincing Chloe to file for divorce.

He was mistaken. Addison would never force a client to do anything. But that fact wouldn't matter much to Michael. He needed someone to blame, and Addison was an easy target.

"I've done everything in my power to keep your new apartment a secret from Michael." Chloe and her six-month-old daughter should be safe. But Addison knew better than anyone that guarantees weren't possible. "Would you be more comfortable staying at a shelter tonight? I can make some calls."

Chloe was quiet for a long moment. Addison pictured the leggy brunette pacing her small apartment. Then Chloe inhaled before letting out the breath slowly. "No. We'll be okay."

"There's no shame in going to a shelter, Chloe. If you're worried—"

"I am worried, but I'm also behind locked doors with a security alarm and the police on speed dial." She let out another long breath. "Seeing him in court today rattled me, and now that the baby is in bed, I have more time to think. It's..."

"Hard to separate the rational fear from the irrational."

"Yes. How long, Addison? How long before I feel safe?"

"A long time."

Years. Maybe more. Addison still carried the scars on her own heart from her failed marriage. "But it gets better. You're a courageous woman, Chloe. And you're building a better life for you and your daughter."

It sounded like the other woman choked back tears. "I don't feel courageous. I feel like a hot mess."

"That's not how I see you. You're a wonderful mom and an amazing person."

The compliments were all true, and Addison made a conscious effort to boost her clients' confidence. It was one of the first things the abuser usually stole.

"Thank you, Addison. I'm sorry to have called so late."

"You can call anytime."

They each said goodbye, and Addison set her phone down on her desk. She rolled her shoulders to rid them of tension. Her home office was decorated in soothing colors of ocean blue and white. A candle flickered on the bookshelf, the scent of vanilla floating in the air.

She'd moved to Knoxville four months ago. The tiny Texas town was an hour outside of Austin. It was close enough she could maintain her law practice in the city but still take advantage of the sense of community she'd been missing in recent years. Her house was a two-bedroom ranch style with pretty shutters and a covered patio.

A bolt of lightning lit up the sky, followed by a boom of thunder. Shelby, Addison's cat, scrambled across the carpet and disappeared down the hall toward the bedroom. The Siamese mix hated storms and had since the day Addison brought her home from the shelter.

"Poor kitty." Shelby had a hiding space under Addison's bed. Chances were, the cat was headed there to wait things out.

Lights flickered. The home security system beeped and then went dark. Addison crossed the room to rearm it. Her fingers flew over the keypad, but nothing happened. Frustration nipped at her. The security company had been out earlier in the week to repair the system. Clearly, it wasn't successful.

A thump came from the rear of the house. Addison froze. Had her cat knocked something over in the back room?

Or was someone in the house?

Her heart rate skyrocketed. Addison held her breath, straining to listen for any sound over the classical music playing on her speakers. Nothing. Indecision waged within Addison. The memory of Michael's glare from court earlier that day rose in her mind. She had a laundry list of clients whose significant others were just as violent.

Silently, on stocking feet, Addison crossed back to her desk. She opened the drawer. A small can of mace rested inside. She wrapped her hand around it. After her ex-husband violated his restraining order and tried to hurt her, Addison had taken boxing and self-defense courses. Ten years of practice had honed her skills, but a real-life confrontation was far different from a controlled environment.

A creak echoed down the hallway. Addison's breath stalled in her chest. She knew that sound well. It came from her bedroom door. The hinges needed oil.

Someone was in the house.

Lord, please help me.

Addison scooped up the cell phone from her desk but didn't pause long enough to call 911. The priority was to get out of the house and to safety. She raced across the living room carpet. Double dutch doors opened to a large backyard and the woods beyond. She could use the trees for cover. Or better yet, she could go to her neighbor's house. Jason was former military.

Addison unlocked the door with trembling fingers. Her thundering heart made it impossible to hear anything. Where was the intruder? Was he coming for her?

Sucking in a breath, she twisted the knob. The door swung open. Frigid air raced over her heated skin. She slipped into the darkness. The lights from her neighbor's house—five yards away—glowed like a welcome beacon.

Something shifted behind her.

Addison whirled. A large figure tackled her and sent her flying. Pain vibrated through her body as she collided with a patio chair. The cell phone and mace flew from her hands. They clattered across the cement and landed in the grass.

She scrambled to get her knees under her. The assailant charged, and Addison lashed out with her foot. It landed in his stomach. He grunted in surprise and backed up a few steps.

She got to her feet and ran. Her ankle throbbed, injured in her tumble with the chair. It hindered her progress. Sucking in a deep breath, Addison screamed, but was cut off as the attacker slammed into her again. They tumbled to the ground. All the air whooshed from Addison's lungs as the weight of the man crushed her.

She shot out an elbow but couldn't get enough force behind the move to make it count.

The attacker slammed a fist into her head. Stars exploded across her vision. His weight was a cement block she couldn't dislodge. Addison's world narrowed to her masked attacker and the frantic beat of her heart. She screamed.

The man's hands went around her throat and squeezed.

TWO

Jason Gonzalez jerked awake as a wet nose nudged his face, but let his eyes drift shut again. He groaned. "What is it, Connor?"

The German shepherd nudged him again. More insistently this time. Jason peeled his eyes open. He'd fallen asleep on the couch with all the lights on. And no wonder. He was exhausted after completing several new paintings for an art show next week in record time. The latest one rested on a nearby easel. The landscape was wintery with snow-capped mountains, bare trees, and a frozen lake. Menacing clouds rolled in from the west, but light still filtered through a sliver of space, cutting a path across the darkness. He called it a Beam of Hope.

Working as an artist had never been Jason's dream career option. No, his goal after leaving the military was to become a police officer. But an IED had destroyed that aspiration. He wouldn't pass the fitness exam now. Still, Jason had fared better than any of the other Marines that day. All the rest had died.

Connor whined. Jason groaned again and sat up. "Okay, boy. Do you need to go out?"

He reached for his shoes. Connor beelined for the sliding doors leading to the porch. His body was rigid, his attention on the yard beyond the glass. A scar ran down the length of his left side, cutting through the fur. Connor had earned his own war wounds as a military-trained bomb-detection dog. Like Jason, he was retired.

The dog whined and shifted at the door. The hair on the back of Jason's neck prickled. The hearing in his left ear was questionable. Had Connor heard something outside? The dog acted as if something was wrong.

Jason shot to his feet, crossed the room, and opened the sliding door. A bolt of lightning lit up the sky, followed by a boom of thunder. Jason gave the heel command to Connor before stepping onto the patio. Woods leading to a state park bordered the edge of his property. It wasn't uncommon for wild animals to wander close to the house while foraging for food. Jason didn't want the dog going after a skunk or some other woodland creature.

Frigid wind rustled the trees, a prelude to the approaching storm. Jason barely felt the cold seeping through his thin T-shirt. He scanned the yard. Motion-detection lights clicked on, illuminating the surrounding area. Nothing stirred. Still, Connor whined next to him.

Jason glanced at the dog. Connor's ears were tilted forward and tension coiled his body. Something was clearly bothering him. "What is it, buddy?"

A scream ripped through the night.

Jason's heart stopped. That'd come from his neighbor's house.

He bolted across the grass, Connor at his side. The properties in their old neighborhood were large. Each house

8

sat on at least an acre. It gave privacy and space, something Jason normally loved. Now it frustrated him. He couldn't get to the other house fast enough.

Jason put more fuel in his legs. His thigh, held together with a rod and pins, protested. Another memento from the IED that'd nearly killed him three years ago. His left side had taken the brunt of the explosion, leaving him with a map of scars etched on his skin and damaged hearing in his ear.

He ignored the bite of pain from his leg, his sole focus on the lights shimmering inside the house. Addison's house. The door leading to the back yard rattled in the wind. Patio furniture was in disarray, chairs knocked over and scattered. Addison was nowhere to be seen.

Where had the scream come from?

Connor growled again, the hair on the back of his neck rising. A bolt of lightning arced across the sky, illuminating the yard and the woods beyond. A man, wearing dark clothes and a ski mask, straddled something.

Not something. *Someone.*

Addison.

"Hey!" Jason raced for them. He gave the release command to Connor, and the dog snarled before barking. The German shepherd burst forward to protect his friend. Connor and Addison adored each other.

The attacker straddling Addison bolted upright. He sprinted for the woods, disappearing into the thick trees bordering the edge of the property. A dirt road was a short distance away. It was rarely used and maintained by the park, a perfect escape path for someone with nefarious purposes. Jason wanted to give chase, but his first priority had to be Addison.

Connor reached the woman on the ground first. His

barking turned to howling. It was a low mourning sound that sent Jason's heart skittering, even as his feet kept moving.

No, Lord, please don't let me be too late.

He slid to a stop next to the prone figure and dropped to his knees. Addison sat up, clutching her throat, her eyes wide with panic, and backed away from him. The terror in her expression cut Jason's heart into pieces.

He lifted his hands in a surrender gesture to avoid frightening her more. "It's me. Jason."

She blinked and seemed to register his presence. "I'm..." Her gaze shifted to Connor. She swallowed, her voice raspy. "He broke into my house."

In the span of a heartbeat, Jason put the pieces together. Addison had tried to escape out her patio door, but the intruder had followed. "Where are you injured?"

"I'm...okay."

It was too dark to see if that was true. Jason glanced at the woods. If the man was willing to attack a woman escaping her home, what else would he do? Would he come back? Jason had learned the hard way never to underestimate the enemy.

"Come on. Let's get you to my house." Hers was a crime scene. Better to leave it untouched for the police.

He wrapped an arm around Addison's slender waist. With ease, Jason helped her stand. Even in the dim lighting, her complexion was pale. Auburn hair swayed around her face, the curls tangled with leaves and grass. She was barefoot.

Tenderness swept over Jason, catching him off guard. Addison had moved into the house next door six months ago, and while they'd struck up an easy friendship, he'd avoided becoming more.

Addison swayed and then sagged against him. Shock? After the ordeal she'd just been through, it was possible.

Raindrops peppered Jason's head as an icy wind skittered across the yard. He didn't have time to help her walk. If Addison was going into shock, the cold wasn't doing her any favors. She needed to be dry and warm. He hooked an elbow under her knees, lifting her into his arms.

Addison's hand came up to clasp his neck. "I...you don't have to..."

She trembled, her teeth chattering.

Jason ignored her feeble protests and started across the yard with quick strides. He was so focused on getting Addison inside, it took several paces before he realized Connor wasn't beside him. He glanced over his shoulder. The dog stood at attention, facing the woods. A low, rumbling growl vibrated his chest.

Jason needed no further convincing. He tightened his grip on Addison and ran.

THREE

Hours later, Addison limped out of the emergency room heading for the hospital exit. The police had taken photographs of her injuries, along with her statement. They'd also taken her clothes as evidence. A kind nurse had rustled up some scrubs, but Addison was eager to change into her own pajamas.

She couldn't process it. The attack. Being strangled. She was no stranger to violence—her ex-husband had broken his vows and struck her—but she'd thought those days were behind her. To be violated again in her own home, a place she'd worked hard to make safe, was devastating.

Don't think about it. Focusing on the assault would make her feel helpless. There was nothing worse. Instead, Addison sent another prayer to the Lord. The small measure comforted her and served as a reminder of her blessings. Things could've been so much worse.

The automatic doors slid open into the hospital waiting room. Jason rose from a chair. He wore cargo pants, a long-sleeved T-shirt, and combat boots. His dark hair was mussed, drawing attention to the curves of his face. The high brow, strong nose, and square chin were well proportioned. Faded scars crisscrossed his left cheek, carving a path from his hairline into the collar of his shirt. They should've detracted from his good looks, but they only enhanced them. Jason was rugged, a warrior, and the scars were a testament to his bravery.

His eyes were the color of warm chocolate. When their gazes met, Addison's heart skittered.

Jason crossed to her. "Are you all right?"

"Fine. Some bumps and bruises, but nothing serious. Thanks to you." Tears welled in her eyes, as the armor she'd wrapped herself in since the attack cracked. "Jason, you saved my life. If you hadn't—"

"The what-if game will drive you crazy, Addison. I'm glad you're okay." His mouth quirked up at the corners. "Besides, it's Connor you should really be thanking. He alerted me to the trouble. Woke me from a sound sleep and demanded to be let outside."

She laughed despite the seriousness of the situation and swiped at the tears on her cheeks. "Good old, Connor. He's my bestie."

"Trust me, the feeling is mutual. Do you know how many times I've had to chase that mutt away from your patio since you moved in? He stares in your windows, hoping you'll sneak him a biscuit. Greedy hound."

"And I thought we were being so covert."

He rolled his eyes. They both chuckled, and the weight pressing down on Addison instantly felt lighter. Jason had that effect on her. His confidence and quiet assurance were comforting. As though his broad shoulders were wide enough to carry any problem until it was resolved.

They hadn't been friends long. She'd moved into the neighborhood six months ago, and Connor's persistence in crossing into Addison's yard had created chances for conversation with Jason. The more Addison learned about the former Marine, the more she found to like. He volunteered at a veterans' hospital, was a talented artist, and had an easy sense of humor. They also attended the same church.

In another time, in another place, she would've been interested in dating Jason. But not now. Friendship was all she could offer. Although Addison longed to one day fall in love again, it seemed an impossible leap. Her heart was still too bruised and broken from her shattered marriage.

Jason tucked his hands in his pockets and tilted his head toward the exit. "Why don't we get you home?"

She nodded, exhaustion seeping into her aching muscles. It'd been a long night. She wanted a shower and her bed, in that order. Addison already knew she'd be sore tomorrow. Her throat felt raw and her ankle throbbed.

Jason offered his arm. "Lean on me. It'll take the pressure off your injured ankle."

She smiled her thanks and slipped a hand in the crook of his arm. Heat radiated from his skin through the soft shirt. The muscle was hard under her palm, and a jolt of attraction arced through Addison. She tamped it down.

"Addison," a voice called out.

She turned. Detective Trevor Whitman strolled toward her from the ER. His sandy blond hair bounced with the force of his gait, and his mouth was tight with worry. Addison groaned inwardly. Trevor's family was good friends with hers, and Addison's mother had been trying to set her up with the detective for ages.

"What are you doing? Didn't the nurses tell you I was coming?" Trevor wrapped his arms around her. "Your mom called and told me what happened. I immediately requested to be made lead on the case and the chief agreed."

Fabulous. Her mom was matchmaking all the way from Florida. Addison had called her parents from the emergency room because her cell phone was damaged during the attack. They would worry if they couldn't reach her. She also hadn't wanted them to hear about the attack through the grapevine. Her parents had moved to Florida last year, but they kept in close contact with many of their friends in Knoxville.

"First, I'm fine." Addison detangled herself from Trevor's embrace. His heart was in the right place, but she'd sensed for a while Trevor was romantically interested in her. Addison didn't want to encourage the notion. "Second, I specifically told my mom not to call you. I don't want to put you in an awkward position with your colleagues. I know detectives can be territorial about their cases."

"Nonsense. Your mom is concerned, and rightly so. It only makes sense I should be in charge of the investigation, given how close our families are. I've already spoken to Chief Walters. The matter is settled."

She debated arguing, but it seemed childish and silly. It was smart to have Trevor on the case. He would do his best to watch out for her, and after tonight, Addison was in no position to refuse the help.

Trevor's gaze shot to Jason. Addison belatedly realized she'd never introduced the two men.

"This is Jason Gonzalez." She gestured toward the former Marine. "He's my neighbor, and the one who rescued me. Jason, this is Trevor Whitman. We grew up together, and our families are close."

Trevor smiled, but it was tight at the edges. No doubt he'd seen Addison holding Jason's arm and misinterpreted the touch. Jealousy didn't look good on him. Still, the detective held out his hand. "It's nice to meet you, Jason. Thank you so much for helping our girl."

She bristled at the endearment and his possessive tone, but discussing it wasn't an option at the moment. Addison wouldn't embarrass Trevor in front of Jason, especially since the two men literally just met.

Jason seemed to sense her tension. He shook Trevor's hand, but his brow furrowed. "I'm glad I was in the right place at the right time. God's providence."

"Right." Trevor dropped Jason's hand and wrapped an arm around Addison before planting a kiss on the top of her head. "I'm so glad you're okay, Addy."

Her heart softened at the catch in his voice. Trevor might push her buttons, but it wasn't something he did intentionally. Since the truth about her marriage came out, Trevor and her family treated Addison with kid gloves. As though she couldn't make good decisions on her own and needed their protection and interference.

It was well-intentioned, but it grated all the same.

She gently pulled away from his embrace. "Trevor, I appreciate that you came down here, but I'm exhausted. Jason is going to give me a ride home, and we should be going."

"You don't need to catch a ride with him, Addy. I'll give you a lift home."

"No, that's okay. Jason's been waiting and we live next door to each other. It makes sense for him to take me."

Trevor frowned, his gaze flickering to Jason, before setting back on her. "Are you sure?"

"Positive. We'll talk tomorrow."

He gave a sharp nod and hugged her again. "I have patrols doing extra rounds at your house tonight. We'll also follow up with the husband of your client. The one you mentioned..."

"Michael McCormick."

"Yep. We'll see if he has an alibi for tonight."

"Thank you, Trevor." She stepped back. "Michael is the first one that comes to mind, but I'll make a list of the others I've received threats from in the last two years. You'll have that in the morning."

Jason's gaze swung to her. "You've received numerous threats? How many?"

She gave him a weak smile. "Too many to count."

FOUR

On the drive home, Jason wrestled with himself. He'd tried —and failed, thanks to Connor—to keep his distance from his beautiful next-door neighbor since she moved in. Since returning from Afghanistan, Jason hadn't felt...whole. It was deeper than the scars etched on his body. It was haunting memories and guilt wrapped up in a package of PTSD. Putting one foot in front of the other took effort on most days, so making new friends required an emotional toll he didn't have the energy for.

Addison slipped past his defenses. She was easy to talk to and quick to laugh. And she loved his dog. It was hard to resist someone who adored Connor.

Now she was in danger. And Jason was smart enough to realize there was no way he would leave her to face it on her own.

He parked his SUV in the garage, got out, and circled around to the passenger side. Addison had fallen asleep on the half-hour drive from the hospital. Long lashes cast shadows on her cheeks. She appeared so peaceful, Jason hated to wake her.

He reached inside the vehicle and gently shook her shoulder. Strands of auburn hair tickled the back of his hand. "Addison. We're home."

She opened her eyes and blinked before focusing on him. Jason was struck with the full force of her beauty. Addison's features were elegant. A slightly turned-up nose, full lips, and porcelain skin. But it was the color of her eyes that fascinated him. They were cobalt blue with flecks of gold and green.

She sat up and rubbed her face. "I was more tired than I thought. Sorry for falling asleep on you."

"No need to apologize. How's your ankle? You probably should've ridden in the back so you could elevate it."

"It's not that bad. It'll be fine in a couple of days."

Jason offered his hand to assist her from the vehicle. Addison's palm was soft, her fingers long and delicate. His heart skipped a beat, but he ignored it. There was no room in his life for a relationship. Not that Addison would see him as anything beyond a neighbor and friend. Jason might have once been attractive, but the IED had destroyed that as surely as it had taken everything else.

"Stay right here a second." Jason dropped Addison's hand. "I've got to grab something from my house and then we'll walk over to yours."

He crossed the garage and opened the door leading to the interior of the house. Connor greeted him with a woof before slipping past to say hello to Addison. Jason went into the adjoining laundry room. Shelby peered out from behind the closed door of a small cat carrier. She meowed in complaint.

"Sorry, girl." He lifted the carrier from the washing machine. "It took longer than I thought."

He carried the cat outside. Shelby meowed again, more

loudly this time. She pressed her furry face against the silver grate and extended a paw through one of the holes. Her claws were extended. Definitely not happy.

Addison's mouth dropped open. "You caught Shelby? Is she okay?"

"She's fine, but the police were going in and out of your house. I didn't want them accidentally letting her into the yard."

"Thank you, Jason." Addison smiled and touched the cat's extended paw. Shelby meowed again, louder this time. "How on earth did you catch her?"

"Treats were involved. Although, honestly, I think she was pleased to see a familiar face."

He offered Addison his arm to lean on, and they began crossing to her house. The thunderstorm had long since passed, but puddles littered the walkway. It smelled like pine and wet grass. The street was quiet. Most people at this time of night were tucked in bed. Chances were the intruder wouldn't come back again tonight, but Jason wouldn't ignore the possibility, no matter how slim. He kept watch as Addison unlocked the front door. Nothing stirred.

Inside the house, Jason did a sweep of each room. All secure.

He joined Addison in the kitchen. She was arming and disarming the security alarm, a frown turning down the corners of her mouth. "I don't get it. How is it possible that one minute it's fine and the next it doesn't work?"

"What do you mean?"

She blew out a breath. "The detective that interviewed me at the hospital said the alarm panel was working when the initial police officers arrived. He seemed to believe I had forgotten to set it and that's how the intruder got in through my bedroom window. But it was set. I know it was."

"Didn't you have a repairman out last week?"

She nodded. "He didn't find anything, but it's been glitchy. All of a sudden the alarm will just fail. That's what happened tonight."

Jason stiffened. Addison caught it and her gaze narrowed. "What?"

He didn't want to scare her, but he also didn't believe in lying. The hesitation must've been written in his expression, because Addison crossed her arms. "Don't protect me, Jason. I might've been a mess earlier this evening—"

"With good reason." Jason didn't want to revisit those harrowing moments after bringing Addison into his house. She'd been pale and shaking but trying to muscle her way through it. "I won't lie. I don't want to make this worse for you."

She jutted up her chin. "Then don't hide what you're thinking."

"Your security system is wireless, which makes it susceptible to being hacked. That could explain why it fails at odd times. Maybe the intruder hacked the system and was testing whether he could make it turn off."

She sucked in a breath. "And when I had a repairman out to the house, he knew it was working and that I'd noticed."

"Yes." Jason's suspicions about the attack on Addison deepened. Whoever the criminal was, he'd broken into her house with one purpose: to kill her. There was no other explanation for chasing after Addison once she escaped the house. And if their theory about the security alarm was true, this attack was well planned. "You mentioned at the hospital you'd received threats over the last few years. Are those in connection to your job?"

She nodded and ran a hand through her hair. It tumbled

around her shoulders in a silky wave of curls. "Representing women against their abusive partners is dangerous work. I've made a lot of enemies over the years."

"This guy you mentioned tonight—"

"Michael McCormick. He's a client's husband." She frowned, her gaze drifting back to the alarm panel. "If you're right, and the security alarm was hacked, someone went to a lot of trouble to get into my house to kill me. That doesn't jibe with a man seeking quick revenge."

Her thoughts echoed his own. Jason leaned against the counter and cleared his throat. "Addison, we've never talked about it, but I've always sensed your work was a calling. I don't want to pry..." His gaze dropped to the bruises on her neck and anger sparked in his veins. "But this attack seems personal. The most likely suspect would be an ex."

Addison closed her eyes. The pain etched on her features made Jason's chest tighten. He wanted to pull her into his arms, but Addison's body was rigid and he wasn't sure an embrace would be welcome. Instead, he gripped the counter and waited her out.

"You'd be right that my career is a calling." She opened her eyes but kept them locked on the tile floor. Addison let out a shaky breath. "But my ex-husband, Greg, died seven years ago of a drug overdose. He can't be responsible for these attacks. And I haven't dated anyone since our divorce."

He pushed off the counter and came to stand in front of her. "I want to give you a hug. Would that be all right?"

Tears shimmered in her eyes. "Don't feel sorry for me."

"Addison, I feel nothing but admiration for you."

He embraced her. The scent of her shampoo circled around him, soft and clean. She choked back a sob, and Jason tightened his arms around her. Addison was a soldier.

Oh, she didn't wear a uniform, but she had a warrior's heart all the same. She provided a voice for those who desperately needed it, and it'd put a target on her back.

Someone wanted her dead and had nearly succeeded tonight. They wouldn't get a second chance.

Jason would make sure of it.

FIVE

Jason stifled a yawn and guzzled his fourth cup of coffee. He'd spent most of the night keeping watch over Addison's house. There had been a time when three hours of combined sleep was enough for the entire day. Not anymore. This morning, Jason felt every one of his thirty-two years.

A short distance away, Connor rolled in the grass before flipping on his side to warm his fur in the sunshine. His brown eyes drifted closed. Lucky dog.

"Could you hand me that screwdriver?" Kyle Stewart asked from the top of the ladder. He balanced a camera in one hand and a handful of screws in the other. "The flathead."

Jason retrieved the item from the toolbox for his friend. "How many additional cameras are we installing?"

"Three. Once the new security system is hooked up, Addison can control it from anywhere. But it's completely hack-proof." He flashed a cocky grin. "Or will be when I'm done with it."

Jason grunted in reply. Kyle was a tech genius and had

been a security specialist in the Army. He was also someone Jason trusted implicitly. They'd become friends three years ago after meeting at the veterans' hospital. The circle grew when Kyle's cousin, Nathan, a Green Beret, was severely injured during a mission. The three men supported each other through surgeries, physical therapy, and readjustment to civilian life. No one understood the challenges better than a fellow brother-in-arms.

Jason took another sip of coffee. "Thanks for dropping everything to take care of this, especially since the ranch is heading into calving season."

The Stewart family owned a sprawling ranch just outside Knoxville. After leaving the military, Kyle and Nathan had thrown themselves into the business. It was hard, dedicated work. Jason spent a week on the ranch last spring while recovering from a follow-up surgery. He'd fallen in love with Kyle's family and the property. The land inspired a series of his most successful paintings.

"I'm glad you called." Kyle screwed the camera in place. His cowboy boots tapped against the metal rungs of the ladder as he climbed down. "There's no reason for Addison to feel unsafe in her own home."

Jason couldn't agree more.

The two men finished installing the cameras and headed inside. The heavenly scents of vanilla and chocolate greeted them. Spread across the kitchen island were enough cookies for a bakery.

"Wow, you've been busy," Jason said.

Addison pulled a fresh tray of cookies from the oven. "The Winter Fair is this afternoon at the church. Several volunteers are making treats to sell, and I'm going to be handling the Dress Drive."

Kyle's brow crinkled. "What's a Dress Drive?"

"We're taking donations for Safe Embrace, a women's shelter in Austin." Addison lifted a cookie off the oven sheet and set it on the cooling rack. "In particular, we're looking for business clothes and dresses appropriate for interviews. Many of the women in the shelter are starting over from scratch. Gaining employment is a big step to their independence."

Kyle reached for a cookie. Addison whacked at his hand with the spatula, but found only air. Jason suspected she'd missed on purpose. Addison hadn't met Kyle before today, but they'd instantly clicked. It wasn't surprising. Kyle never had a problem attracting women. His Southern drawl and charm made him easy to like. But the playful banter between Addison and Kyle left Jason feeling like a third wheel.

It was something he didn't want to think about. He and Addison were just friends. That's all they would ever be, and if she wanted to date Kyle, then it was her right. Jason had no claim on her.

Kyle held up the cookie he'd stolen and grinned broadly, the dimple in his cheek winking. "These are amazing."

Addison glared at him, but there was no actual heat behind it. "You've had half a dozen already. At this rate, I won't have enough for the church."

"You heard the woman." Jason pointed at the laptop waiting on the kitchen table. "We've got work to do."

"Yes, but a man needs sustenance to do his best." Kyle bit into the cookie before pulling out a kitchen chair. He set up the new security system and then showed Addison how to use it. "Once you get your cell phone replaced, I can connect that as well. You'll be able to see the cameras from anywhere."

She bit her lip, twisting a dish towel between her hands. "And no one can hack the system?"

"I've double encrypted it. It's not fool-proof, but it's as tight as a home system can get."

She let out a breath, and the tension in her shoulders dropped. "Thank you, Kyle. I can't tell you how much I appreciate this."

Addison went around the kitchen island and retrieved a takeaway container from the pantry. It was full of her home-made cookies. She handed it to Kyle. "These are for you."

Kyle grinned and then hugged her. A jolt of jealousy shot straight through Jason and his body stiffened. It was a ridiculous reaction. He took a deep breath and forced himself to relax.

Kyle shot him a curious look over Addison's shoulder before releasing her and backing off. "Thanks, Addison."

She spun on her heel and grabbed another container of cookies, handing it to Jason. "And these are for you. Cookies are a poor substitute for saving my life and arranging for a new security system, but I promise it's the first batch of many."

Warmth spread through him. He met her gaze. "I told you, thanks isn't necessary."

"Maybe not." She stood on her tiptoes and hugged him briefly. "But it makes me feel better."

Jason's heart skipped a beat, and a blush heated the back of his neck. He mentally berated himself. There was nothing to her gesture other than simple kindness. Hadn't she also given Kyle cookies and a hug?

Thankfully, Connor nudged Addison's hand and distracted her. She rubbed his ears and fed him a dog biscuit.

They chatted for a few more minutes before the men

cleared out of the house so Addison could finish getting ready for the Dress Drive. Jason closed the back door and Kyle fell into step beside him as they crossed the yard. Connor joined them.

"You like her." Kyle arched his brows. "I caught the look on your face when Addison hugged me."

Nope. Jason wasn't going there. "Of course I like her. She's nice."

His friend snorted. "That's not what I meant and you know it. But I can also tell you don't want to discuss it, so I'll leave it at that."

"Praise the Lord for small miracles."

Kyle laughed, but then his face grew serious. His gaze swept the woods. "Did you attempt to retrace the attacker's steps after the police were done searching the area?"

"I did, but if there were any tracks, the thunderstorm washed them away. Probably what he was counting on." Jason glanced back at Addison's house. "He used the thunder to mask the sound of him breaking in. If things had gone as planned, it would've prevented anyone from hearing her screams as well."

Kyle's jaw tightened. "She outwitted him by escaping."

"That's my guess. But the attacker caught up to her in the doorway. In his attempt to subdue her, he pushed her into the patio furniture. The noise alerted Connor." Jason went into his house and booted up the computer. It was already connected to the big-screen television. "There's something I want to show you. The attacker took out Addison's security system so we don't have footage of the assault. But her system records for a week before taping over itself. I was going through the days prior to the attack and found this vehicle on the street."

He played the security footage. An older model SUV

came into the shot and slowed outside Addison's house before speeding up again. It had a decal on the windshield. The driver's face wasn't visible through the darkly tinted windows.

Jason hit pause. "I showed this to Addison, but she didn't recognize the vehicle. It doesn't belong to anyone on this street. That much I know for sure. The footage is grainy and there isn't a clear shot of the license plate. I've sent it to the police, but they have a backlog at the lab. Could you clean it up? Even a partial license plate would help."

"It'll take some time." Kyle squinted at the image frozen on the television. "And I make no promises. The quality of the video is terrible."

"Understood. The driver came around several more times on different days, always at night."

Jason showed each video clip to his friend. Kyle's expression darkened, and he rocked back on his heels. "This isn't a onetime thing. He's going to try again."

"This feels personal to me, so yes. I believe he'll try again." Jason crossed his arms over his chest. "I want him caught before he can."

SIX

Three hours later, the Winter Fair was in full swing. Sunshine spilled across the church parking lot. Screams of joy from the children in the bouncy castle mingled with the scent of popcorn and hot chocolate. Booths and tables created a path for visitors to follow. Local residents were selling everything from handmade quilts to peach preserves.

Addison made sure no one was watching and lowered the collar of her turtleneck shirt. Rachel Harrison, her friend and paralegal, winced. "Oh, Addy. That's awful."

"It looks worse than it feels. The doctor said the bruising should disappear in a week. Truth is, I'm thankful. Things could've been so much worse."

"It was fortunate Jason and Connor intervened." Rachel tugged on the end of her french braid before tossing it over her shoulder. "I've spoken with everyone else at the office. None of them have been followed, and no one recognized the SUV in the video you sent."

"That's a relief." Addison had forwarded the surveillance video of the SUV to her coworkers. She worked at a nonprofit that aided domestic abuse survivors. If the attack was connected to her job—a client's spouse bent on revenge—anyone at the office could be a target. "Still, everyone should be extra cautious until the police catch my attacker."

"I've made that clear. Have the police spoken to Michael McCormick?"

"I don't know. I'm heading over to the station for an update after the event is over. Trevor should be there."

Rachel blew out a breath and picked up a donated suit jacket. "To be honest, I'm hoping Michael is your attacker. Is that awful?"

"If it is, you and I are in the same boat."

Addison didn't want to consider the alternative. Last night's attack was horrible, but it was the hacked security system and the surveillance video of the SUV passing by her house that truly spooked her. Did she have a stalker? If so, was he here now? Watching her?

A shiver raced down her spine.

The crowd parted. Jason strolled toward their booth. His thermal shirt molded to the muscles in his biceps and stretched across his broad chest. Connor marched at his side. Jason had offered to attend the Winter Fair with Addison to protect her. It was a thoughtful gesture, and she had to admit, having him close eased her anxiety. Maybe it was wrong, but she felt safe with him in a way that defied logic.

He'd saved her life, which instantly bonded them, but it was deeper than that. Telling Jason about her ex-husband had been difficult. Addison rarely shared the information with others. Too often people were judgmental or pitying. Both reactions were hard to take. But Jason had been understanding. Kind.

His response had brought the entire evening's

emotional toll to a boil, and Addison hadn't been able to stop herself from weeping. Jason's embrace had been tender and comforting. The memory heated her cheeks. Addison hid the color in her face by greeting Connor with enthusiasm. She scratched the dog behind the ears. His tongue lolled out.

Jason tucked his hands in the pockets of his cargo pants, his gaze skipping over the booth. "Y'all got a lot of donations."

Addison nodded. "I know. Isn't it great? These dresses and suits are going to make a big difference to the women at the shelter. Having the right clothes for an interview seems like a minor thing, but it matters. The church said they're planning to host the Dress Drive every year."

A woman drove up. Rachel bustled over to collect the donated garments, waving off Addison's offer to assist. From the way she hugged the driver, Rachel was friends with her. The two women started talking.

Addison offered Jason a bottle of cold water from a cooler under the table and then opened one for herself. It didn't escape her notice that Jason's body was positioned outward, his gaze constantly scanning the crowd. She kept her voice low. "Do you think he's here?"

"I haven't noticed anything strange."

The tension in Addison's spine relaxed. Maybe their suspicions were wrong, and the attack was a one-off. She took a sip of her water. The cool liquid soothed her sore throat. "Thanks again for arranging the new security system. It was nice to meet Kyle. Were you guys in the military together?"

He shook his head. "Different branches. We met in the VA hospital, shared the same room. Then Kyle's cousin, Nathan, was injured while on a mission overseas. The three of us grew tight, helping each other through physical therapy and stuff."

She smiled. "That's nice."

"It is. They're great guys. I'd trust them with my life."

High praise coming from Jason. He was selective about his friendships. It was a trait Addison could appreciate. After her divorce, she'd also been slow to develop new relationships. It was hard to be open and vulnerable when you didn't feel normal.

"What time are you going to the police department to get an update from Trevor?" Jason asked.

"In an hour." She gestured to the racks of clothes. "We're going to pack up and load these into Rachel's vehicle. She's dropping the donated items off at the shelter on her way home."

"I'll do a perimeter check and then come back to help load up."

"Thanks, Jason." Addison patted Connor on the head. "See you soon, boy."

Rachel hurried over carrying several garments on hangers. "Addy, some of these clothes are gorgeous. Look at this suit with the jewel neckline."

Addison set down her water bottle to help her friend. They hung the clothes on the rack and oohed and ahhed over the recent additions.

Rachel tapped her head with the heel of her hand. "Oh, I'm such a dunce. The church secretary stopped by while you were assisting someone else. There are more dresses in the storage room. Some people couldn't make it today but still donated items. Can you tell me where the storage room is? I'll go get them."

Addison frowned. The storage room was near the offices and troublesome to find if you didn't know the church layout. "No, you stay here. I'll go get them." She craned her head, but Jason was lost in the crowd. "If you see Jason, let him know where I am."

"Oh, I'll be sure to." Rachel shot her a mischievous grin.

Addison rolled her eyes, even as a flush crept over her cheeks. "Don't start. Jason and I are just friends." She scooped up her water bottle. "I'll be back in a few minutes."

She weaved her way through the crowd, waving at a few neighbors here and there. She drained the last of her water and tossed the bottle into a recycling bin. The main entrance to the church was unlocked. Addison slipped inside. The door closed with a click behind her and sounds from the Winter Fair became muffled.

Her tennis shoes were silent on the carpet. She located the storage room and flipped on the lights. Dresses hung from a rack off to the side. Addison collected them, then closed the door firmly behind her. Should she lock it—

"You sent the police to my house."

She spun. Michael McCormick stood at the end of the hallway. His posture was rigid. A red flush stained his cheeks and his eyes were bloodshot.

Addison's stomach clenched. She gripped the dresses tighter as sweat coated her palms. There was no point in responding to Michael. He was here for a confrontation. She had no intention of giving it to him.

She darted away from the storage room, but Michael stepped into her path, blocking her escape. "Who do you think you are? Sending the police to question me?"

Addison jutted up her chin. "Let me pass, Michael."

Her voice came out strong, belying the trembles coursing through her. Addison forced herself to meet his gaze. Dark circles shadowed the skin under his eyes, and the malevolent twist of his mouth iced her blood. He wanted to hurt her.

She could scream, but would anyone hear her? This section of the church was empty. Everyone was outside. And Michael blocked the only exit.

"You aren't going anywhere until you admit to lying." He stalked closer. Michael jutted a finger toward her. "I never threatened you. Not once."

Addison's heart rate skyrocketed. Sweat dripped down her back. She'd left her mace in her purse back at the booth. *Think, think.* Addison imagined the layout of the hall in her mind. She took two steps back and her hip bumped into a small, wooden table. The dresses fell from her arms. They scattered on the floor in a pool of color.

"Michael, listen to me." She reached back until her fingers brushed against glass. A lamp. She followed the curved shape until she got to the narrow top. "Threatening me won't help prove your innocence. You need to leave me alone."

His face turned a deeper shade of red, and he took another step forward. "Don't tell me what to do."

Addison gripped the lamp in her hand and poised on the balls of her feet, preparing to swing in self-defense. Michael wanted to hit her. His fists were already clenched. Two more steps and he'd be close enough to harm her.

"Back off, Michael, and let me out of the hallway." She glared at him, forcing any shred of fear from her voice. "Now."

SEVEN

Raised voices came from the hallway near the church offices. One of them sounded like Addison. Jason mentally berated himself for leaving her alone even for a moment. He picked up his pace, Connor by his side. They rounded the corner to find a man yelling at Addison.

Michael McCormick.

Jason recognized him from the photograph on his company website. Gone was the smooth professional with the polished suit and slicked-back hair. Now Michael's face was mottled with rage and his fists were clenched. His muscular frame towered over Addison, who was leaning against a small table. Her expression was hard and determined, but her complexion was pale. She was terrified.

A white-hot rage burst through Jason's veins. "Get away from her."

Connor growled, as if to punctuate his master's order. The German shepherd stayed by Jason's side, but the hair on the back of his neck rose.

Michael glanced over his shoulder and his bloodshot eyes widened. He immediately took several steps away from

Addison and raised his hands in the classic sign of surrender. "Hold on. It's not what it looks like."

"It looks like you're threatening her." Jason placed his body between Michael and Addison. Without taking his eyes off the man in front of him, he asked, "Addison, are you okay?"

"She's fine," Michael snapped. "I didn't do anything to her."

Connor bared his teeth. The dog was too well trained to attack without an order, but that wouldn't prevent him from making his presence known. Jason took half a heartbeat to spare a glance behind him. One of Addison's hands clutched a lamp from the table. Faint trembles shook her shoulders.

Fury at Michael's behavior mingled with the desire to pull Addison into his arms. Jason kept both emotions in check. "Addy, you okay?"

She nodded and released the lamp. "He didn't touch me."

He'd scared her though. Jason's gaze swung back to Michael and his fingers twitched with the desire to give the bully a taste of his own medicine. He resisted. Not for Michael's sake. For Addison's. She had a history of interactions with violent men—first her husband and then some of her clients' exes. Jason would never do anything to frighten her.

Michael tugged on his shirt and puffed out his chest. "I told you, I didn't do anything to her. I'm here to clear up a misunderstanding."

Jason bit back the retort hot on his tongue, but Connor had no compunction about making his feelings known. He growled low in his throat.

The smirk fled Michael's face, and he took another step

back. "Keep your dog under control. I've got something to say."

Addison shifted until she was at Jason's side. "What do you want, Michael?"

"You accused me of being the one who attacked you last night." Michael pointed a finger at her. "You and my wife are busy spreading rumors and lies about me. I won't stand for it."

"I didn't accuse you. The police are questioning several individuals."

He snorted. "Yeah, right. I'm no dummy. My wife is looking for a big payout in the divorce. If I'm arrested for assault, it makes Chloe's case more convincing to the judge."

Addison frowned. "I'm sure your attorney has advised you that Texas is a common-law state. You don't have a prenup with Chloe. Everything you acquired after you got married will be split between you."

"Yes, but the judge doesn't have to divide it equally. I built my business from nothing. If you think I'm going to give Chloe one red cent—"

"Enough." Addison bent and picked up a dress from the ground. "We shouldn't be having this conversation. Call your attorney, Michael, and talk to him about it."

"I already have. He believes we can keep Chloe from getting anything. That's why you cooked up this ridiculous accusation about me. Like I said, if I'm arrested for assault, Chloe's accusation that I beat her looks legitimate. The judge will side with my wife."

Addison lifted her chin. "I don't need to make up false allegations about you. The photographs of Chloe's injuries are proof enough of what you did to her."

"She did that to herself. Fake injuries to go along with

her fake claims. I never laid a hand on Chloe, and I didn't attack you either." His lip curled with disdain. "This scheme won't work. I have an alibi for last night."

Jason arched a brow. "Where were you?"

"It's none of your business. You aren't the police." Michael's glare shifted to Addison. "Stop conspiring with my wife against me or else."

Jason crossed his arms over his chest. "If you're attempting to prove your innocence, threatening Addison isn't the best way to do it."

A red stain crept up Michael's neck and into his cheeks. "If I wanted her dead, she'd already be six feet under."

Charming. Jason's patience was reed thin. Michael's behavior toward Addison was hostile. It left little doubt of his capability for violence. The businessman could definitely be behind last night's attack.

Jason jerked his chin down the hall. "You've said what you came to. It's time for you to go."

Michael's gaze narrowed, and he puffed out his chest as if preparing for a fight. Jason nearly laughed. He could take the man down in two seconds even with his war wounds. Once a Marine, always a Marine.

"Go ahead, take a swing." Jason hardened his tone, letting anger bleed into his voice. "But my guess is you won't. Bullies like you never want to take on someone their own size."

Michael's gaze skittered away, and then he smirked. "You aren't worth it."

The words came out whiny. The man was a coward. A niggle of doubt wormed its way through Jason's convictions about Michael's guilt. Approaching Addison in the church hallway was reckless. Last night's attack, however, had been well planned. The two didn't mesh well.

Connor growled as if to remind everyone of his presence. And his loyalty to Jason.

Michael took several steps backward down the hall. "Make sure that dog stays there. If he bites me, I'll sue you." He paused at the end of the hallway. "And I mean it, Addison. Don't accuse me of anything else. You don't want to make me mad."

Addison glared at him but said nothing. Once Michael disappeared around the corner, she set the dresses on the table. "Come on. We should follow him to see what kind of vehicle he drives. I want to know if it's the same SUV that was circling outside my house."

They quickly exited the church. Throngs of people were weaving a path along the booths. Michael was heading for the overflow parking. Jason grabbed Addison's hand to prevent them from being separated in the crowd. She interlocked their fingers, and Jason couldn't help but notice how soft her skin was.

Wrong time, wrong place, Gonzalez. Focus.

He kept Michael in view but maintained enough distance so the other man wouldn't realize he was being followed. The crowd thinned.

Jason widened the gap. "Where's he going?"

"There's additional overflow parking for the fair behind the bakery," Addison said. "He should turn at the next street if that's where he's headed."

As she predicted, Michael turned. Jason increased his pace to keep from losing the other man. They rounded the corner of the building and the overflow parking lot came into view, but it was devoid of people. Jason paused on the street, scanning the area. "Where'd he go?"

Addison squinted against the sun's glare and then

pointed. "There he is. He must've parked at the edge of town."

A dark-haired man disappeared around the corner of an abandoned store. Jason hurried to catch up. He didn't want to lose Michael without seeing his vehicle. If Michael was driving the same SUV that had circled outside of Addison's house in the days prior to the break-in, then chances were, he was also the attacker.

The street was empty. This area of town didn't have much foot traffic, especially now that the Winter Fair was in full swing. Jason kept his senses alert, watching for any signs of trouble. He wouldn't put it past Michael to ambush them.

Next to the abandoned store, Connor sniffed the air and stopped dead in his tracks. He whined. Jason's heart skittered, and he yanked Addison to a stop.

"What is it?"

He barely heard her question. His gaze was locked on Connor. The dog backed away from the store and gave two quick barks, as if signaling danger. He didn't want to go past the abandoned store...

Jason sucked in a sharp breath. There was no time to explain, no time to second-guess. He shoved Addison in front of him, using his body to shield her. "Run. Run."

She took off without question. Jason followed, keeping his body between Addison and the store. Connor led the charge down the street.

An explosion erupted behind them.

EIGHT

The acrid scent of smoke lingered in the air. Broken glass littered the sidewalk, sparkling in the sun. Firefighters sprayed water on the last of the flames in the abandoned store while police officers kept townsfolk behind the yellow crime-scene tape.

Addison leaned against a patrol car. Every muscle in her body hurt. The explosion had knocked her to the ground, but Jason had used his body to shield hers from the falling debris. He'd saved her life. Again.

Jason stood a short distance away, giving his statement to a police officer. His thermal shirt was torn at the sleeve and a scrape marred the curve of his cheek, but he was otherwise unharmed. A miracle considering how close they'd been to the explosion.

Addison's gaze drifted to the commotion in front of the blown-out store. Trevor was in deep discussion with Police Chief Robbie Walters. The chief was in his mid-fifties with thinning salt-and-pepper hair. His face, weathered from time in the sun, wore a perpetual frown. Or maybe it only seemed that way to Addison. The chief liked to rub elbows with the mayor and city council members. He saved his charm and smiles for them.

She shifted her attention to the abandoned store. Lingering whiffs of smoke drifted on the wind and bits of twisted metal mingled with the glass on the sidewalk. Addison trembled. No one had been seriously hurt or killed. But they could've been.

Connor sat next to her. The dog pressed his body into hers, as if he could sense her emotions. She placed a kiss in between his sweet brown eyes and then stroked his head. "You're such a good boy. I'm going to make you homemade dog biscuits. No more of those store-bought ones. And I promise to grill a steak for you once a week."

A set of familiar combat boots appeared. "You'll spoil him."

Addison's heart skipped several beats at the rich timbre of Jason's voice. She lifted her head to meet his gaze and had the insane urge to launch herself into his strong arms. "What's wrong with spoiling him? Connor smelled the bomb inside the store and warned us. He saved our lives."

Connor's tail swiped across the ground and his tongue lolled out in a doggie grin. Jason chuckled and patted his head. "Okay, okay. I agree. Steak every week."

Addison's gaze drifted toward the commotion near the store, an icy knot in her stomach. "How did Michael know we would follow him to the parking lot?"

"I'm not sure. Have you gotten in contact with your client, Chloe?"

"Yes. I've explained the situation and warned her to be extra careful." Addison rubbed her forehead. "Trial for their divorce has already begun. It's set to conclude on Tuesday. If Michael is the one behind this, he's going to get increasingly desperate."

"Is this just about his business? Or is there more to it than that?"

"This is about money." Addison's nose wrinkled. "Michael never mentions his daughter. He doesn't even want visitation. All he cares about is keeping Chloe from getting her fair share of their assets."

"How much money are we talking about?"

"Chloe is set to receive two million dollars in the divorce."

Jason whistled. "Well, that's a lot of motivation." He frowned. "What I don't understand is why Michael would come after you? Chloe could simply hire another divorce attorney."

"But another attorney wouldn't help her the way I have. Michael's convinced the reason Chloe won't go back to him is because of my involvement."

"So if he gets you out of the picture…"

"He can convince his wife to return to him. Or take a deal for less money." Addison gave in to her desire and took a step forward, dropping her forehead to Jason's broad chest. "What kind of madman plants a bomb to kill me? People could've been seriously hurt. Not just you and me. Other townsfolk."

"God was watching over us." Jason wrapped his arms around her. "You aren't in this alone, Addy."

His embrace was firm and comforting. Addison sank into it, hot tears springing to her eyes as her emotions welled. She didn't know why this was happening to her, but she was grateful for Jason's friendship.

"Thank you, Jason." She lifted her head. "For everything."

He swiped at the tear coursing down her cheek. "We'll figure this out. I promise."

Her breath caught at the tender brush of his thumb across her skin. Her gaze snagged his, and the emotions reflected in his dark eyes erased the coldness seeping into her bones. She knew Jason would protect her with his life. He was a good man.

Warning bells clanged in her head. Since her divorce, Addison had avoided any kind of romantic relationship. Her heart was battered and bruised, and she wasn't sure she could fully trust someone again. Jason was nothing like her ex-husband—of that she was certain—but could she invest in something new? Was she ready? Addison wasn't sure.

Someone nearby cleared his throat. Addison turned her head.

Trevor, decked out in his police uniform, stood a short distance away. He was staring at them, a scowl etched on his features. "Sorry to interrupt, but I need to speak to you both."

Addison eased from Jason's embrace, a flush heating her cheeks. There was no reason to be embarrassed. She was a grown woman, after all. But Trevor had always been like a protective big brother and old habits were hard to break. She straightened her shoulders. "What is it?"

Trevor fixed his gaze on her. "The fire captain will do a preliminary investigation after the structure is deemed safe, but at this point, there's nothing to indicate a bomb caused the explosion. According to the store owner, the county has been out several times to fix a leaky gas line but have been unsuccessful."

"It was a bomb," Jason said. "I'm certain the investigation will prove it."

"How can you be sure?"

"Because Connor told me." Jason gestured to the German shepherd at his side. "He's trained in bomb detection. Connor's retired from the military, but his skills don't disappear."

Trevor's nose wrinkled slightly, and he appeared less than impressed. Addison crossed her arms over her chest. "Jason's right. If Connor hadn't alerted us to the bomb, we'd both be dead now. Have you questioned Michael McCormick?"

"No. Mr. McCormick was questioned about the attack against you last night, but he has an alibi for the time in question."

"Where was he?"

"At a party. At least 100 guests were in attendance, including the mayor of Austin." Trevor placed a hand on his duty belt and the leather creaked. "Michael cannot have been the man who attacked you last night. And right now, we have no proof that what happened at the store was a bomb. Nor can we connect the two incidents."

Addison huffed. "You've got to be kidding me, Trevor. Last night someone tried to kill me, and today, I just happened to be next to an exploding building. That's a strange set of coincidences."

"I understand, but I can't operate on hunches. What you and Jason think, what the dog says..." He cast a derisive look in Connor's direction. "It doesn't matter. I need hard evidence and facts. I don't have them."

This conversation wouldn't get them anywhere. She knew Trevor well enough to know he'd made up his mind. "How long will the investigation into the explosion take?"

"A few days, minimum. More likely a week or two."

She could be dead in a week or two, at this rate. Addison blew out a breath. "You'll let me know what the fire captain finds."

"Of course." Trevor tilted his head to the side. "Addy, can I talk to you for a second? In private?"

She followed him a short distance away. Once they were out of earshot, Trevor placed a hand on her shoulder. "I'm sorry. I know you're unhappy with Michael's alibi, but I promise, we're taking the investigation into your attack seriously. I have officers running down the other names on the list you gave me. We'll find something."

His words and assurances tempered her frustration. Trevor wasn't being illogical. He had to operate on facts. But she still didn't like the way he dismissed Jason's conviction about the cause of the store's explosion.

"Keep an open mind, Trevor. I believe the explosion was caused by a bomb. Whoever is doing this is dangerous and needs to be stopped."

"He will be. I promise." He squeezed her shoulder. "But I also want you to keep an open mind. The break-in at your house and the explosion today probably aren't connected."

A sharp retort lingered on her tongue, but she swallowed it back down. There was no point in arguing. "Listen, Trevor, if that's it, I'd like to go. I have a headache and I'm in desperate need of a shower."

"Sure." He dropped his hand. "Why don't I come by tomorrow morning and pick you up for church? We can join my family for lunch afterward. My parents would love to see you."

"Thanks for the offer, but I'll stick close to home tomorrow. I can attend church service online." She offered Trevor a weak smile. "It'll give you guys time to figure out what's going on."

He rocked back on his heels, and for a moment, Addison thought he would argue. Then he nodded. "Okay. Call me if you change your mind."

"I will, thanks."

She turned to leave, and Trevor called her name, stopping her. She paused.

"I'm here, Addy. For anything you need." He lifted his gaze to hers. "You can always count on me."

A pinch of guilt plagued her. It was obvious Trevor had romantic feelings toward her, feelings she didn't share. It would be so much easier if she did. He was a handsome guy with a caring demeanor, and their families were close. On paper, they would make a great couple. But Addison had learned the hard way forcing a relationship was a mistake.

It could leave you bleeding and bruised.

NINE

The explosion, and the conversation with Trevor, left Jason with a sour taste in his mouth. He spent most of the night keeping watch over Addison's house between bouts of fitful sleeping. Nightmares stalked him. At dawn, he gave up on getting any rest at all and started praying.

Lord, have I been arrogant? Am I a fool to believe I can protect Addison?

The incident in Afghanistan haunted Jason. He and Connor had been sweeping the outside of a building when the explosion happened. A car bomb. The vehicle had been parked on the street between several others. The explosion had shattered Jason's world in less time than it took to draw a single breath. Three of his teammates died.

Mentally, Jason could accept it wasn't his fault. He'd been following protocol. But emotionally...the what-ifs plagued him.

Why, God? Why? And what do I do now?

The answer to his last question was simple. Unavoidable. Jason couldn't leave Addison to fend for herself. The threats against her were increasing. Trevor didn't seem to accept or understand the gravity of the situation. It didn't matter if Jason was nervous about protecting Addison. He didn't have a choice.

A Marine always answered the call to duty.

Connor whined and nudged Jason's arm. Then the dog licked his elbow. Connor had an innate ability to read Jason's emotions. He was more than a companion; he was a fellow soldier and survivor.

Jason stroked Connor's soft fur. "Don't worry, buddy. We'll keep her safe. I know how much you care about her."

He didn't want to think about—couldn't even consider—how much he cared about Addison too.

A knock came on his front door. Jason rose and crossed the room on quick strides. A glance through the window confirmed his suspicions. Kyle and Nathan stood on his porch.

Jason opened the door and greeted his friends. "We don't have long to chat. We're supposed to report to Addison's house immediately for breakfast before church service. What have you found out about Michael McCormick?"

After speaking with Trevor, Jason took matters into his own hands. First, he contacted his friend, Texas Ranger Grady West. Grady made a phone call to the Knoxville Police Department offering his help on the case. The chief of police refused. Without hard evidence there was corruption or some kind of cover-up going on, Grady couldn't force matters. Texas Rangers could only work specific cases dictated by statute or by invitation from local law enforcement.

Jason's next calls were to his military buddies. Nathan and Kyle were experienced soldiers with extensive training. Gathering intel on Michael—and any other suspects that arose—was child's play for them.

Nathan's mouth was set in a grim line. "Michael doesn't drive an SUV with a decal in the front. In fact, he doesn't have an SUV registered to him at all. He owns a Tesla and a Land Rover. I also verified his attendance at the party. His alibi holds."

"So maybe Michael isn't behind the attack against Addison after all." Jason frowned. "Addison created a list of other people who've made threats against her. I think we should do a preliminary check on them too. I don't want to miss anyone."

Nathan nodded. "I'll start on it today."

Kyle tucked his hands in his jacket pockets. "I'm still working on the surveillance video. You should have it by tonight." He tilted his head, his steady gaze locking on Jason. "How are you doing? After yesterday?"

After the bombing. Jason could lie, but there was no point. These were his friends. If anyone could understand what he was going through, it was Kyle and Nathan.

Jason blew out a breath. "She could've died, guys, and I led her right into the danger."

"Baloney. Addison was the one who suggested following Michael to his car." Kyle lifted his brows. "If you hadn't been there with Connor, she wouldn't have known about the bomb."

"Kyle's right," Nathan said. "You saved her life. God placed you right where you were needed."

Were his friends right? Had God placed him in Addison's life to protect her? Jason hadn't considered it from that point of view, but maybe he should.

"Come on." Jason held the front door open long enough for Connor to slip out. "Let's get over to Addison's. She's got breakfast waiting for us."

"Breakfast." Nathan rubbed his hands together, a broad

smile on his face. The former Green Beret could eat his way through a buffet and still have room for more. "Now you're speaking my language. What kind of breakfast?"

Jason shrugged. "Not sure. But try to leave some for the rest of us, will ya?"

"I make no promises."

Kyle shoved his cousin down the porch stairs and the two men started wrestling. Jason tripped them both and then jogged ahead to Addison's door, chuckling. His buddies caught up to him. A wrestling match ensued. Petty insults and childish comments upped the ante.

A sharp whistle brought all three men to a halt. Jason's head was trapped underneath Kyle's armpit. He craned his neck to find Addison standing on her front porch. An apron hugged her slender waist and her long hair was pulled back into a low ponytail.

She attempted a stern expression, but a smile played on her gorgeous lips. "Would you gentlemen kindly stop fooling around in my front yard for all the neighbors to see?" She shook her head. "Worse than children."

Kyle chuckled and released Jason's head from under his arm. Then he followed up the move with a shove.

Jason pinwheeled but stayed upright. "I'm going to sic Connor on you."

Kyle ignored him, bounding up the steps to greet Addison. "Sorry about that, Addy. Won't happen again." He flashed her a charming smile before jerking a thumb toward Nathan who was retrieving his hat from the grass where it'd fallen during the wrestling match. "That lump over there is my cousin. I'm not responsible for his table manners."

Addison bit her lip hard and it appeared she was doing her absolute best to keep from laughing in Nathan's face. He tipped his cowboy hat in her direction. "Pleasure to meet you, ma'am. Nathan Hollister. Thank you for inviting us to breakfast and church service."

"My pleasure." She gestured toward her open door. "Please, go on inside and make yourselves at home."

Kyle and Nathan disappeared into the house. Jason took the porch steps two at a time. "Hey. Sorry about that. My friends are a handful."

"They're wonderful."

Addison's smile made Jason's breath quicken, but the dark circles under her eyes didn't escape his notice. She hadn't slept well either. Not that he could blame her. She'd been attacked twice in two days.

A trace of flour crossed her cheek. Without thinking, Jason reached up to swipe it away. The curve of her cheek was smooth, like satin, with a faint smattering of freckles dancing across the surface.

She laughed and swiped at her face. "I must look a fright. I'm a messy chef, but I promise the food is good."

"You look beautiful. As always."

The words were out of his mouth before he could snatch them back. Heat flooded the back of his neck, and he wanted the porch to open up and swallow him whole. He was normally reserved. What was it about this woman that cracked all his defenses?

Addison lifted her gaze to meet his and her smile widened. "Are you flirting with me, Jason?"

He cleared his throat. "I'm paying you a compliment, hoping you'll forgive me when we get inside and discover Nathan has eaten everything already."

She laughed. Jason let out the internal breath he was holding. Crisis averted. He needed to remember that he and Addison were friends. That's all they would ever be. Jason was damaged goods. Romance and falling in love was impossible. The sooner he accepted that, the better.

Addison glanced inside and the smile melted from her face. "Before we join Nathan and Kyle, I have a favor to ask."

"Anything."

"I spoke to my client, Chloe, this morning. She's very upset about the attacks, especially when I mentioned Michael had an alibi. She asked me to come by her apartment. I think she wants to tell me something but doesn't feel comfortable sharing it over the phone. Will you go with me to see her?"

"Of course." He was grateful she asked. Jason didn't want Addison going anywhere by herself, given the attempts on her life. "We can go right after church."

TEN

Chloe McCormick lived in a three-story apartment complex within walking distance of downtown Austin. The building desperately needed some maintenance along with a fresh coat of paint, but there was a solid attempt to make it family-friendly. Younger children played on a well-tended playground and several older kids skateboarded across the parking lot.

Jason followed Addison up a set of rickety outdoor stairs. The metal groaned under his weight. He had visions of them plummeting to their death. "This staircase leaves a lot to be desired."

"I know." Addison shot a glance over her shoulder as she rounded the landing to the second floor. "The building is run-down, but the people living here are great. It's mostly families, and they watch out for each other. Chloe doesn't have much personal money. Almost everything is tied up in the divorce."

Jason had done enough research on Michael McCormick to learn the man was ruthless. In business and, it seemed, personally as well. How did a man turn out his wife and child to fend for themselves on their own? Then again, Michael was an accused wife beater.

"Chloe's employed across the street." Addison paused on the second-floor landing and pointed to a nearby church. "She works for the daycare, in the baby room. It's a blessing because she can take her daughter to work with her."

"How old is her little girl?"

"Stella's nine months." Addison started climbing to the third floor. "Chloe left her husband when she was three months old. Michael found a dirty dish in the sink and beat Chloe within an inch of her life."

Jason's blood heated. "Did she press charges?"

"She did. They're pending. Michael's gone on a media blitz to convince people Chloe is lying in order to get her hands on his money. It's baloney, but the campaign against her is working. Most of her friends don't speak to her anymore."

"That's why he was so angry with you yesterday."

She nodded. "A disgruntled wife is easy to dismiss, but it's a lot harder to overlook a second woman coming forward to say Michael is violent."

Addison reached the landing, slightly out of breath. Jason joined her. His gaze swept the parking lot below. Everything seemed fine. Jason had taken evasive maneuvers to ensure no one followed them to Chloe's apartment, but he wouldn't let his guard down for a moment.

"Everything okay?" Addison asked, stepping to the edge of the railing. "What is it?"

He shook his head. "Nothing. I'm just being cautious."

"Oh." She let out a breath and the tension in her shoulders relaxed. "You'll tell me if there's something to worry about?"

"Absolutely." Jason smiled to reassure her.

He followed her to the apartment at the end of the corridor. Addison knocked. The sound of rock music filtered through the closed door. The volume fell instantly, as if someone had rapidly turned the dial down. Jason didn't hear footsteps, but he had the feeling Chloe was peering through the peephole in the door.

A second later, locks snicked. The door opened revealing a slender woman with a baby on her hip. Chloe's dark hair was pulled away from her face and secured at the sides. She was makeup free and barefoot. The baby—Stella —resembled a chubby cherub. She chomped on a biscuit.

"Addison, hi." Chloe gave her a one-armed hug. "Thanks for coming by. How are you?"

"I'm doing okay." Addison gestured toward Jason. "This is the neighbor I told you about, Jason Gonzalez."

Chloe hefted the baby higher on her hip before extending a hand. "Of course. Nice to meet you, Jason."

"Likewise." He shook her hand. "Your daughter is beautiful."

"Thank you. I think she is too." Chloe's smile widened, but it didn't erase the worry lingering in her eyes. She stepped back, holding the door wider so they could enter. "Please, come on in."

The apartment was a tiny one-bedroom with an open floor plan. It was decorated minimally. The couch was a futon with a removable cover and there was a small end table on either side. Photographs of Stella at various stages of development had been framed and hung on the wall. There was no television. A playpen rested in the corner and toys were scattered on the floor.

"Can I get either of you anything to drink?" Chloe moved toward the kitchen. She hefted Stella higher on her hip again. "I have iced tea, coffee—"

"I'm fine." Jason stepped over a ball. "But thank you kindly."

"Nothing for me either, Chloe." Addison smiled at her client.

"Please, sit." Chloe waved toward the couch before settling on the floor with the baby. Addison joined her, picking up a rattle and waving it for Stella. The little girl grinned and crawled toward her.

Jason took a seat on the futon. The mattress was more comfortable than he expected.

Addison picked up Stella and tickled her belly, causing peals of laughter from the baby. "I swear she's grown since I saw her last and that was only a week ago."

"I know. She's getting so big." Chloe's face softened when talking about her little girl. It was clear she adored her. "Stella tried to lift herself out of the crib this morning. I have to lower the mattress."

"It won't be long before you're running." Addison tickled the baby again. "Isn't that right, Stella?"

Jason didn't think his esteem for Addison could be any higher, but watching her now, it grew. There was nothing fake about Addison's interaction with her client and the baby. She genuinely cared about them. It probably made her a fantastic lawyer. Chloe was lucky to have Addison on her side.

Chloe's gaze darted to Jason, and the softness in her expression morphed to concern. She absently picked at a loose strand on a soft baby book. "Addison, I'm worried about you. First the break-in last night and then the bombing yesterday. I know Michael had an alibi for the break-in, but I still believe he's behind this."

"Why?" Jason asked.

"For starters, my husband has a special fascination with

bombs. He's read books about them and he has friends in the police department. One of them is a bomb technician. Michael had him for dinner once." She licked her lips, glancing at Addison. "He blames you for the divorce. He's convinced that you talked me into it and I believe he wants revenge."

Addison shook the rattle for Stella again. "Michael has an alibi for the break-in at my house."

"I know, but he's rich enough to hire someone. My husband is ruthless and very smart. He knows how to work the system to his advantage." She swallowed hard. "Like I said, he has friends on the police force."

Which meant Michael was familiar enough with police investigations to create an alibi for himself. He was also worth several million dollars. Chloe was right that he had enough money to hire a hit man. Jason leaned forward. "Do you have any idea who your husband would hire to attack Addison?"

"No, but it has to be someone he already knows. Michael wouldn't risk hiring a stranger."

Jason made a mental note to look into Michael's employees. "Would you be willing to tell the police this information?"

"I already have." Chloe continued to pick at the loose thread on the baby book. Her movements were growing increasingly frantic. "I spoke to Detective Trevor Whitman this morning. He didn't seem to take what I had to say seriously. That's not surprising. My husband is friends with the Knoxville police chief. What's his name again?"

"Robbie Walters," Addison said.

"Yes, that's it. My husband also knows the mayor of Knoxville." Chloe's expression was bleak. "Michael uses his friendship with powerful people to protect himself."

Jason didn't like this. Trevor hadn't taken them seriously about the bomb yesterday and he'd been quick to dismiss Michael's potential involvement. Was that because of Chief Walters's friendship with Michael? He hated to think the police were compromised, but why else would they ignore evidence?

He removed his cell phone from his pocket and pulled up a still photograph of the SUV from Addison's surveillance video. Jason showed it to Chloe. "Have you ever seen this vehicle before?"

She studied the photograph carefully and then shook her head. "Sorry, no."

Addison's mouth flattened into a thin line. "Someone from the Knoxville Police Department told Michael about the surveillance video and our suspicions about the SUV. That's how he knew we would follow him out to the parking lot yesterday. The confrontation was a setup."

Stella crawled over to her mother. Chloe pulled the baby into her lap and kissed the top of her head. "I'm so sorry, Addison. I never meant to put you in danger."

"You have nothing to apologize for. This isn't your doing. If Michael is behind this, he's responsible for his own actions."

Chloe nodded. "Please be careful, Addison. Once Michael decides something, there's no changing it. He's also vicious." She shuddered. "He'll keep coming after you, no matter what it takes."

ELEVEN

Addison jerked awake, heart thundering, with a scream posed on her lips.

She blinked. The nightmare faded as the familiar furniture of her own bedroom came into focus. She sucked in a breath. Then another. Sweat coated her brow and her hands trembled. A paperback book rested on the bed next to her, tangled in the sheets. She must've fallen asleep while reading. The events from the last few days had finally caught up to her.

It was dark outside her window. A quick glance at the clock confirmed it was nearly eight. Addison swung her legs over the side of the bed, groaning as her muscles protested the movement. Shelby yawned and picked her way across the bed. She rubbed against Addison, purring.

"I bet you're hungry, sweetie. It's past dinnertime." Addison stroked the cat, letting the soothing motion erase the lingering side effects of the nightmare. Shelby's purr grew in intensity. "Come on. Let's see what we can scrounge up in the kitchen."

It wouldn't be much. Addison hadn't gone to the

grocery store in over a week. She also didn't feel up to cooking. It was on nights like this she pulled out her favorite childhood sandwich, peanut butter and jelly. Not very mature, but it hit the spot.

A night-light in the kitchen glowed. It was bright enough to see, and since Addison's eyes had adjusted to the dark, she didn't bother flipping on the main lights. Shelby twirled between her legs, loudly meowing for her meal. Addison maneuvered around her. "Okay, okay. It's coming."

She quickly opened a can of cat food and dumped it in Shelby's bowl. The cat pounced on her food like she hadn't eaten in a week. Addison chuckled. "No one will take it away from you, I promise."

The motion-detection light on the back patio lit up and a dark shape moved across the kitchen tile. Addison's heart dropped to her feet and then jumped into her throat.

Someone was in her yard.

She ducked behind the safety of the island. Her phone and mace were in the bedroom. Since the confrontation with Michael yesterday, she'd been keeping both close to her at all times. Disorientation from the nightmare had muddled her brain. She'd forgotten the items on the nightstand.

A scrape came from her patio, the sound of a boot against the concrete. Addison muffled a shriek. She reached above her head to the block of knives on the counter. Her hand wrapped around the hilt of a butcher knife. She pulled it free.

The shadow reappeared on the kitchen tile. Large enough to be a man. Would he try to break in? Her gaze shot to the alarm panel next to the door. The light glowed green, showing it was armed. There was a panic button, but she would have to leave the shelter of the island to hit it.

Another panel was in the living room. And her bedroom. But the island was in the middle of the kitchen and there was a wide open space between Addison's hiding place and the doorway. If the intruder had a gun, she didn't stand a chance.

Addison held her breath, waiting. More scrapes came from the patio. What was he doing? Looking for a way in? She peeked around the corner of the island. A face appeared in the window above the door.

Addison screamed.

"Addy, it's me. Trevor."

She placed a hand over her racing heart and sagged against the island. The relief was short-lived, as anger took hold. Addison shot up from behind the island, disarmed her alarm, and unlocked the back door. "What on earth are you doing? You scared the living daylights out of me."

A sheepish look came over his face. "Sorry. I wasn't sure you were awake." He gestured to the dimly lit kitchen behind her. "I sent a text, but you didn't answer. All of your lights were out and you've had a rough couple of days."

"Most people knock on the front door."

His brows arched. "Most people haven't known you since diapers. Can I come in?"

"I'd rather you not." Addison's tone was sharp, but she didn't care. Trevor had no business creeping around her yard, no matter how long he'd known her. Especially given the threats. He was a police officer and knew better.

Addison stepped onto the back patio and shut the door behind her. The cold air raised goose bumps on her skin. "What is it, Trevor?"

His gaze narrowed. "I've never known you to be rude, Addy. Is someone in the house with you?"

By someone, he meant a guy. The comment did nothing

but fuel her temper. She crossed her arms over her chest and gave him a pointed look. "No one is in the house with me, not that it's any of your business. It's been a long day, however, and I'm tired. What is it?"

He shrugged. "I just wanted to check on you."

"I was hoping you had an update on the case. My client, Chloe, called and spoke to you this morning. She's convinced her husband is involved."

Trevor rubbed the back of his neck. "I know, but Michael has an alibi."

"She believes he may have hired someone."

"Addy..." Trevor dropped his hand and shifted his feet. "Chloe is a disgruntled wife in the middle of a nasty divorce and child custody suit. She has a reason to lie."

"I can't believe you just said that." Addison straightened to her full height. The threads of control on her temper threatened to snap. "Chloe isn't a liar. There's a police report, Trevor, proving her allegations of abuse. Michael nearly killed her. He was arrested and charged."

"That's not the same thing as being guilty and you know it. He still has to go through a trial to be convicted. Come on. You know how this works. You're a lawyer." Trevor shook his head. "Jason is putting ideas into your head. When did the two of you become so cozy, anyway?"

"Jason has nothing to do with this, and no one is putting ideas in my head." She glared at him. "I'm beginning to think there's a reason you won't investigate Michael McCormick. Is the Knoxville Police Department compromised?"

Trevor's mouth dropped open, and a flush heated his cheeks. "You've got to be kidding me? Are you accusing me of being a crooked cop? I thought you knew me better than that."

"Someone told Michael about the SUV in the surveillance video. That's how he knew we would follow him out to the parking lot. The confrontation at the church yesterday was a well-planned attack. Michael planted that bomb."

"There's no proof there was a bomb."

Trevor practically shouted the words. He seemed to catch himself before he could say more, spinning on his heel to march the length of the porch. Addison let him cool down for a few moments before saying, "Don't yell at me, Trevor."

The command was self-assured. It'd taken Addison a long time, along with years of therapy and prayer, to learn how to stand up for herself. She used those hard-won skills to fight for her clients in the courtroom. Tempers flaring no longer scared her, although it was never Addison's intention to escalate a disagreement that far.

Trevor paused a short distance away. "I'm sorry for losing my temper. I shouldn't have yelled, but it hurts my feelings that you think I would ever go against my oath as a law enforcement officer."

"I'm sorry too. I didn't mean to hurt your feelings, but Michael McCormick is friends with both the mayor and Chief Walters. Whether or not you realize it, there are powerful people protecting him."

"What has gotten into you, Addison? You're accusing a man of murder. That's not something to say lightly."

"I'm not saying it lightly. Michael threatened me, Trevor."

"It was unwise of him to confront you, but that doesn't make him a killer. Why are you so convinced Michael is behind the break-in?"

Her cheeks heated. Trevor made it sound like she was

being unfair, when all she was asking was for the investigation to be thorough. "Why are you so convinced he isn't?"

He threw up his hands. "He has an alibi, Addison. And there is no evidence he hired anyone. Michael is a successful businessman. It would be reckless to kill you. Michael may be many things—including a hothead—but he's not stupid."

"You talk as if you know Michael McCormick personally." An unwelcome thought slithered through her mind. Trevor was about the same height and size as the man who'd attacked her a few nights ago. Addison took an instinctive step backward. "Do you?"

Trevor was silent. The porch light cast shadows on his face, morphing it into something ugly. Unfamiliar. Fresh goose bumps prickled Addison's skin and her breath stalled. No. Trevor couldn't be her attacker.

Could he?

TWELVE

Addison stood in her driveway and waited until the tail lights from Trevor's vehicle faded. She wrapped her arms around her midsection. Their conversation had left her jittery and confused.

She glanced at Jason's house. The lights in the living room glowed softly. Before thinking too much about it, Addison crossed the grass and stepped onto his front porch. Wind chimes danced above her head. She rang the bell.

Connor woofed seconds before the door swung open. Jason was dressed for comfort in sweat pants and a T-shirt. A dish towel was slung over one muscular shoulder. "Addison, come in out of the cold. Is everything okay?"

"Not really. No." She crossed the threshold and wiped her feet on the entrance mat. The warm scent of meat and garlic teased her nose. Addison's stomach growled. "I'm sorry. Am I interrupting your dinner?"

"Not at all." He closed the door and indicated she should follow him through the house. The living room held oversized leather couches and a big-screen television. An open floor plan provided a view of the kitchen. "I'm making beef stew, but it needs longer to cook. Have you eaten? I have plenty."

Her cheeks flushed with embarrassment. The impromptu decision to drop in had been a mistake. Jason had done enough for her already. It was bad manners to push her way into dinner with him as well.

Connor nudged her hand and Addison absently petted his head. "The offer is very kind, but I should've called or texted first."

"Friends don't need to call or text before coming over. At least, mine don't." He flashed her an easy smile. "I come from a big family and never mastered the knack of cooking for one. You'll be doing me a favor by staying for dinner. Otherwise, I'll be eating beef stew for a week."

She laughed, leaning on the bar separating the living room from the kitchen. "When you put it that way, how can I refuse?"

"Good. Now, what's wrong?"

Addison quickly recapped her conversation with Trevor. "I feel terrible saying this, but Trevor is the same height and weight as the man who attacked me. Does that sound paranoid?"

"No. Gut feelings shouldn't be ignored." Jason was quiet for a long moment. "You know Trevor better than I do. Do you think he's capable of violence?"

"I think everyone is capable under the right circumstances." She sighed. "But no. Trevor and I are childhood friends. He's never been violent. However, he is ambitious. It's no secret Trevor wants to be Chief of Police one day. Michael's connections to the mayor and Chief Walters complicates matters. Trevor won't rock the boat for fear of losing out on his chance of climbing the ranks."

"In other words, he can't be trusted."

"Yes." Her nose wrinkled. "As much as I hate to say it, I don't think we can rely on anyone in the police department. Trevor isn't the only one with ambition. Chief Walters has discussed running for the state legislature. I heard a rumor last week that he's putting a campaign together, although nothing has been officially announced."

"I heard the same. Unfortunately, ambition and a friendship with Michael aren't enough to prove a cover-up."

"Especially since Michael has an alibi for the night of the break-in." She rubbed her forehead. "I don't know. Maybe Trevor was right and I'm making connections that aren't there. Michael could be innocent. He's not the only man I've ever made angry."

"You aren't wrong to be cautious. If it makes you feel better, I've had the same thoughts. I even called a friend of mine with the Texas Rangers."

"You did?"

Jason nodded. He used a serrated blade to cut two slices of thick bread. "Grady offered to assist with the investigation, but Chief Walters refused his help. It could be simply that the chief wants to keep control of this case. Or it could be he's covering up for Michael. Either way, I think you're right. We need to operate as though the chief is compromised."

It was a terrible position to be in. Addison valued law enforcement. Most of the officers she'd worked with were honest people. "So what do I do now? Launch my own investigation?"

"Kyle is cleaning up the image of the SUV from your surveillance video. If we can get a clear view of the license plate, or even a partial, that would provide a new lead. In the meantime, Nathan is digging into Michael along with the other men on the list you provided to the police who have threatened you in the past."

"Oh, Jason...I appreciate the help. Truly. But I don't know if it's a good idea to involve Kyle and Nathan."

His mouth quirked up. "Nathan and Kyle have faced down some of the most dangerous terrorists in the world. Trust me, Michael McCormick and the other bullies on your suspect list don't scare them."

He didn't say it, but Addison heard the words all the same. Jason wouldn't be scared away either. The knot of worry eating away at her stomach lining uncoiled.

She shook her head and chuckled. "How do you make everything seem easy, even when it isn't?"

He winked. "Military training 101. Never let them see you sweat."

They both laughed.

There was nothing more to do at the moment. The last few days had been hectic and stressful. Maybe it was time to give the case a rest. She leaned over the edge of the counter. "Can I do anything to help with dinner?"

"Nope. It's almost ready. Would you like some iced tea? Or I have soft drinks."

"Iced tea would be fantastic."

Addison's attention shifted to the dining room. It'd been converted into an artist studio. Canvases rested on easels. More were on the floor. A long table took up one wall and held clear organizational drawers filled with brushes and painting supplies. "I haven't asked how things are going with your artwork. Don't you have a show coming up soon?"

"In a few weeks. I've finished all the paintings for it."

She drifted into the studio, stopping before a gorgeous painting of brilliant colors. A river flowed around large rocks before cascading into a waterfall. Something about it looked familiar, but she couldn't place why. "Is this painting of an actual place?"

"Niagara Falls." Jason joined her, close enough she caught a whiff of his aftershave. Something spicy and clean. "This is what it looks like when you skydive over the area."

"You went skydiving?" She shuddered. "No, thank you. I'm terrified of heights."

He chuckled. "It's not for everyone."

"Your paintings are beautiful and lifelike." She'd looked up the cost of his paintings once. They sold for a small fortune. "Did you always want to be an artist?"

"No. Painting was a hobby until I was injured in Afghanistan. Then it became an outlet. Recovering from the IED explosion took a long time. Physical therapy, surgeries....it gives you too much time to think."

There was an underlying sadness buried in his voice. Addison knew several of Jason's comrades had died in the explosion that'd nearly killed him and Connor as well. He rarely spoke about it, and she didn't want to push. "When did you start selling your paintings?"

"While I was still in the hospital, a doctor asked to purchase one. Little did I know, her father was the fourth richest man in the US. My career took off after that. I decided it was God's way of intervening in my life. My artwork brings joy to people, but it also lets me give back to the community."

Jason never bragged, but Knoxville was a small town. He donated a lot of money to various charities, such as the library, after-school programs, and the veterans' hospital. She admired the way he'd turned a tragedy into purpose.

She elbowed him gently. "My dad used to say this phrase to me whenever life got hard. Triumph over adversity. That's exactly what you did."

"I didn't do it alone. God was with me the whole way."

"He always is." Addison stopped in front of an unfinished painting of a little girl. She appeared to be about five or six and was running through a field of flowers. Behind her, dressed in a military uniform, was a man. "This is stunning."

"That's my goddaughter, Maddy, and her biological father. Marcus and I met during basic training and grew close. He died while on deployment. It's a long story, but Maddy was adopted by a wonderful woman named Tara. She's married to the Texas Ranger I mentioned earlier, Grady. They've become my close friends." Jason's gaze drifted over the painting. "Maddy doesn't have any photographs of her dad, so I wanted to give her something to remember him by."

Addison's heart squeezed tight. Jason had to be one of the most thoughtful men she'd ever met. Everything about him drew her closer. His strength, his kindness, his innate goodness. But now wasn't the time to muddle things with romance. The focus needed to be on finding the man who was trying to kill her.

After that...well, Addison would cross that bridge when she got there.

THIRTEEN

Forty minutes later, Addison threw her head back and laughed. Auburn curls spilled over her shoulders and her eyes twinkled. Had Jason ever seen a more beautiful woman? If so, he couldn't remember.

"So here is Kyle carrying this pitiful kitten he rescued from the trash can while on a walk around the VA hospital grounds." Jason cupped his hands together to demonstrate how small the cat was. "And oh, she was smelly. So what does he do? Kyle tucks the kitten into his jacket in order to sneak it into the hospital for a bath. Except the minute he steps into the room, a doctor shows up to check the stitches on his leg."

Her eyes widened. "No."

"Yes. And Kyle still has the kitten in his jacket. He lifts his leg so the doctor can check the stitches, and everything was going okay, until the kitten started meowing."

"Hold on," she said, between giggles. "This story can't be true. How did Kyle explain the meowing to the doctor?"

"Tummy upset." Jason shook his head. "The doctor

didn't buy it for a minute, I'm sure. Neither did the nurses. Everyone ignored the obvious signs that Kyle had snuck a kitten into his hospital room. Ms. Whiskers lived with us for three days before Kyle was released."

Addison wiped at the water gathering in the corner of her eyes from laughing so hard. "I love it. I'm going to tease Kyle about this the next time I see him."

"You should have dinner with us sometime. Kyle, Nathan, and I get together at a diner every Wednesday. The food is good, but we really go there for the desserts. The apple pie is out of this world."

"Sounds wonderful. I'd love to come." She glanced at her empty bowl. "Speaking of good food, the stew was amazing."

"Thanks. It's my mom's recipe."

Over dinner, they'd each talked about their respective families. Their experiences couldn't have been more different. Addison was an only child whose parents were still happily married. Jason was one of five kids and his dad had died when he was a teenager. Despite that, Addison and Jason shared similar values, rooted in faith and family.

"Are you still hungry?" Jason asked. "Would you like some more?"

"No, I couldn't eat another bite." She collected his bowl and stacked it on top of hers before carrying the dishes to the sink. "I'll clean up."

"No way, Addy. You're my guest."

"Don't even try to stop me." She tossed him a heart-breaking smile. "You've saved my life twice and cooked dinner. Loading your dishwasher is the least I can do."

They joked and laughed while cleaning. The more time Jason spent with Addison, the harder it was to keep his distance. But becoming romantically involved with her was out of the question. The scars on Jason's body were nothing compared to the ones on his heart. War had changed him. Permanently. He suffered from nightmares and guilt. Addison deserved so much more than he could give her.

She flipped off the faucet and wiped her hands on a dish towel. "This was fun. Next time, you can come to my house and I'll cook."

"I was hoping you would say that." He winked. "Beef stew is the only dish I know."

They both laughed. Jason's phone beeped with an incoming text from Kyle. The warmth of the evening faded as reality came crashing down. His phone beeped again, this time with a photograph. It was a still image of the SUV. The driver and license plate were still blurry, but the decal on the front windshield was clear. It was a gremlin holding a cigarette.

"What is it?" Addison asked.

"Kyle cleaned up the video of the SUV as much as he could. He sent me a photograph." Jason handed her the phone. "Do you recognize the vehicle?"

Her complexion paled. Jason took her elbow, afraid she might pass out, and steered her into a chair. Addison covered her mouth with her hand, horror filling her eyes as she stared at the photograph. "I think...this could be my father-in-law's car. He had a decal like that." She blew out a breath. "But I can't be sure."

Jason sat in the chair next to her. "What's your father-in-law's name?"

"Wendall Atkin." She closed her eyes as if she was trying to picture something in her mind. Addison shook her head slightly. "I can't be sure this SUV is the same as his. Wendall's vehicle was new, and I only saw it once. He came to my office shortly after Greg died and we had words."

"About what?"

"Wendall blamed me for my ex-husband's death." She drew in another breath and seemed to grasp hold of her runaway emotions. Addison set the phone down on the table. "In order to understand, there's some history I need to tell you."

Jason nodded. He could sense this was going to be difficult for Addison. She never talked about her marriage, and he knew firsthand what it was like to examine a painful past.

"I was in my last year of law school when Greg and I met. He was ambitious and charming. Smart. He'd already graduated and was working at one of the most prestigious law firms in Austin. We started dating and everything seemed perfect. In retrospect, there are things about him I should've noticed early on, but I was naïve."

"What kind of things?"

"Greg was possessive and jealous. It's hard to explain, unless you've been in a similar relationship. It's a slow progression. Greg would drop subtle hints that no one loved me the way he did. He called often, checking to see where I was and who I was with."

She rubbed her thumb over her wedding ring finger. "Greg proposed the day after I graduated. I was over the moon. We married quickly. Too quickly. Another red flag I should've paid attention to." Addison bit her lip. "The first time he slapped me was on our honeymoon."

Jason's gut clenched tight, and it took every ounce of control to keep his posture relaxed as a rush of anger burst in his veins. The idea of anyone hitting Addison...it caused a protective surge Jason had never experienced before. "How bad did it get?"

"Bad. I made a lot of mistakes, Jason. I should've left

him the first moment he struck me, but Greg cried and apologized afterward. He swore it wouldn't happen again. I took my marriage vows seriously and thought we could work through it." She continued rubbing her ring finger. "But the more time passed, the more difficult it became. We settled into a vicious pattern of dysfunction, and I was ashamed to tell anyone what was going on."

He placed a hand over hers, stilling her movements. "I hope you still don't feel that way."

She raised her head and their gazes locked. Tears shimmered in her eyes, and they shattered Jason. He wanted to take away every ounce of her heartbreak. "You didn't deserve what happened to you, Addy. None of it."

"Thank you for saying that. It's taken me a long time to heal. I still don't know if I'm there."

That was a feeling Jason was very familiar with. It struck him then how alike he and Addison were. Both of them were struggling to move on from a painful past. But now wasn't the time to think about that. He gently squeezed her hand. "How long were you married?"

"A year. Greg pushed me down the stairs and put me in the hospital. I filed for divorce and got a restraining order against him. The police arrested Greg for assault." She blew out a breath. "He was convicted. The law firm fired him. Greg started abusing drugs and alcohol. He went into a downward spiral. Nine months after our divorce, he died of an overdose."

Jason sat back in his chair. "His father blamed you for what happened."

She nodded. "Wendall showed up at my office, yelling and screaming about how I murdered his son. But that was seven years ago and I haven't heard from him since. I can't believe he would come after me now."

Jason could. Blame could twist into a need for revenge that grew over time. "Do you know where Wendall lives now?"

"No." She released his hand and picked up the phone, studying the picture. "But I know someone who may."

FOURTEEN

The next morning, Jason plugged an address into his GPS. Addison sat in the passenger seat beside him. The scent of her shampoo teased his senses. It reminded him of oranges and lazy summer days. He inhaled deeply, drawing the fragrance into his lungs, and then mentally berated himself. After dinner, Jason had spent most of the night convincing himself to keep Addison squarely in the friend zone. Anything else would only lead to a broken heart.

Two minutes in her presence and he'd already failed miserably.

The GPS displayed the best route. It would take twenty minutes to get to their destination. Although the sun was shining, storm clouds hovered in the distance like a bad omen. Jason's hand hesitated on the gear shift. "Are you sure it's a good idea to visit your former brother-in-law, Addy?"

"Positive. When I texted Steven early this morning, he was happy to hear from me. He said to stop by the construction site he's working on." She dug around inside her purse and removed a pair of sunglasses. "Steven may not be in touch with his dad—there was some bad blood between them—but he can provide insight into Wendall's thinking. He'll know if his dad is holding a grudge against me."

Jason was uneasy about bringing Addison around anyone related to Wendall, but it wasn't his call. Addison made her own decisions. He needed to trust her judgment. And in the off chance she was wrong, Jason would be there to keep her safe.

He backed out of the driveway, and within five minutes, they were on the highway. Jason kept watch to make sure no one was following them. "You mentioned there was bad blood between Wendall and Steven. What happened?"

"It wasn't one thing. Steven was ten when his parents divorced. He was very close to his mother. I don't think Steven and Wendall ever got along. There was abuse in the home."

So Wendall was violent. That was another tick against him. "What about Steven and Greg?"

"There was no love lost between them either. They're actually half-brothers. When I filed for divorce, Steven supported me. He was the only one from Greg's family to do so. We don't talk often, but we've kept in contact over the years."

Steven sounded like he had his head on straight. That eased some of Jason's concerns. He followed the GPS instructions to a house under construction. From the size of the structure, it would be a mansion. A pile of bricks sat under a tarp next to a cement truck. Workers in hard hats and dirty jeans unloaded equipment from a black pickup truck. Atkin Construction was written on the side.

"There's Steven," Addison said, gesturing to a bulky man in a white hard hat.

Unlike the workers, Steven was dressed in a polo shirt

and carried a roll of architectural plans under his arm. His face was clean-shaven, but his work boots were scuffed and worn.

Steven spotted them and headed in their direction. "Addy, hey." He hugged her, but the embrace was distant and distinctly brotherly. "Nice to see you. It's been a long time."

"It has." Addison touched Jason's arm. "This is my friend, Jason Gonzalez."

Steven smiled broadly. "Hey, man, nice to meet you."

"Likewise."

Jason shook Steven's proffered hand. His grip was firm, but not bruising. Everything about the man bled confidence without arrogance.

"Sorry about making y'all drive down here to meet me." Steven tilted his head toward the unfinished house. "The weatherman is predicting rain for the next few days and we're on a deadline."

"It's not a problem." Addison smiled. "I'm glad to see your business is doing so well."

"Thanks, Addy. Now tell me, what's going on? Your text said it was important."

Addison quickly ran through the recent attacks. Steven's brow furrowed and his muscles tightened. The plans under his arm became crumpled. Everything about his reaction conveyed surprise and concern, yet something was off. Jason couldn't put his finger on what though.

"An SUV was seen passing outside my house a few days before the break-in." Addison showed Steven a photograph. "Do you recognize this vehicle?"

Steven's expression hardened. "That looks like my dad's SUV. Addy, I'm sorry. I should've called the minute Wendall got out of prison."

Jason's spine stiffened. "Wendall was in prison? For what?"

Steven's gaze shot to the workers. None of them were within earshot. A saw whirred and the repetitive jolt of a nail gun drifted across the construction site. Still, Steven took a step closer and lowered his voice. "Murder. My dad killed the man who was with Greg on the day he died."

Addison inhaled sharply. "Why didn't you tell me about this?"

Steven removed his hard hat and swiped at the sweat beading on his brow. "I thought you knew. The murder happened in Austin. I just assumed—"

"You were wrong. I didn't know Wendall had killed someone. Where is he now?"

"No idea. I haven't seen or spoken to my dad in nearly six years. Not since he was arrested for killing Greg's friend. Our relationship wasn't good to begin with, and then he committed murder. I mean..." He swallowed hard. "I'm ashamed to be related to him."

Jason could sympathize. Sometimes coping required burying whatever had happened and moving forward as if it didn't exist. Otherwise, it could drown you.

"When was Wendall released from prison?" he asked.

"Three months ago. He only served six years." Disgust crossed Steven's face. "Wendall took a plea deal, and the prosecutor reduced the sentence since the man my father killed was a known drug dealer."

Jason didn't like it, but he knew such deals were common. Still, six years for premeditated murder seemed ridiculous. "Why did Wendall kill him?"

"Revenge. He blamed the man for Greg's death. Greg and this friend were partying, and Greg overdosed. He might've survived if the friend had called 911."

A cold sense of dread washed over Jason. "What about Addison? Does your dad also blame her for Greg's death?"

"He does." Steven removed the plans from under his arm and attempted to reshape them. "If you're asking whether my father could be behind these recent attacks, my answer is a resounding yes."

Addison trembled. It was faint and Jason only noticed because he was standing so close to her. He placed a hand on the small of her back. A subtle reminder that she wasn't in this alone.

She leaned into the touch but kept her gaze on Steven. "Do you know where Wendall is? How can we find him?"

"I don't know, Addy. Like I said, I haven't seen or spoken to my dad since his arrest. About a month ago, a couple of police officers showed up at my office looking for him. Apparently, Wendall skipped out on his parole officer. There's a warrant for his arrest." He shrugged. "My best guess is that he's hiding somewhere, but I couldn't tell you for sure. You could try talking to some of my dad's family members. His sister is still alive and living in Austin. She may know more."

Jason showed him the picture of the vehicle again. "Are you certain this is your dad's SUV?"

"Not 100%, but Wendall had a decal on his windshield just like that." Steven squinted as he studied the picture. "Same placement and everything."

"He owned this vehicle before the murder. Wendall had to store it somewhere while he was in prison. Any idea where?"

"Nope, but my dad had a bit of money. He could've placed his vehicle in a storage unit while he was in prison. Or a family member may have held on to it for him."

"It's been eight years since Greg died." Addison licked

her lips. "Do you think your dad would come after me now?"

"Yes, I do. Wendall always had a vengeful streak. My dad never cared much about me, but Greg was different. Wendall would walk over hot coals barefoot for his firstborn son." He snorted. "They were a lot alike, Greg and Wendall. Cruel. Abusive. They deserved each other."

There was a hint of jealousy buried in Steven's voice. Did he have a need for his dad's approval, even if the man was a criminal?

Steven's gaze flickered to the workers before focusing back on Addison. His expression was grim. "Wendall got caught for murder once, but he's had several years in prison to plan. Don't underestimate him, Addy. If he wants you dead, Wendall will keep coming for you until the job is done."

FIFTEEN

Sweat dripped down Addison's back. She punched the boxing bag in front of her and the vibration from the impact sang up her arm. She followed it with two more sharp jabs before stepping back. Her chest heaved with the exertion. "I needed that."

"I'm sure you did." Lisa Morales, Addison's best friend, released the bag to let it swing. "You've had a rough couple of days."

The noise of people talking and the clank of weights filtered through the closed wall of their private room at the gym. Lisa owned the business and ran the boxing classes. Addison had considered skipping her regular workout, but the gym catered to women clientele only. There was no reason to believe she'd be unsafe.

Addison undid the strap on her boxing glove. She tucked the glove under the opposite arm and yanked. Her hand, covered in protective tape, popped free. "I didn't realize how weak the attacks made me feel. It's nice to remind myself that I'm strong."

"You *are* strong." Lisa placed a comforting hand on her

elbow and met her gaze. "Not just physically. Emotionally too."

Sudden tears sprang to Addison's eyes. Lisa had been her best friend since grade school. There wasn't anything they hadn't been through together. "What would I do without you?"

"You'd be fine. I'd be a disaster though. Who else would come to watch my little monsters at the drop of a hat?"

Addison laughed. "Your kids are the best. I love babysitting."

It was true. Lisa had two rambunctious, sweet little girls. Two years ago, Lisa and her husband, Damon, went through a difficult divorce. Damon had fallen into substance abuse after injuring his back at a construction site. He refused rehab. Lisa was brokenhearted but took steps to shield her girls from their father's increasingly erratic behavior. Addison had done everything possible to help her good friend through a difficult time, including watching the girls whenever Lisa needed to work late.

Lisa frowned and turned Addison's arm. She winced at the bruises caused by the tumble into the patio furniture. "Oh, Addy, this looks painful."

"It looks worse than it is, promise." She tugged her shirt-sleeve down to cover the marks. A quick glance in the full-length mirror on the far wall confirmed that sweat had erased the makeup covering the fingerprint marks on her neck. She absently touched them. "Jason stopped the attacker before he could do any real harm."

"I'm so thankful he was there. At the break-in and the store explosion. To think of what could've happened..." She shuddered before grabbing a towel from her bag and patting her brow. "What's the story between you and Mr. Tall, Dark, and Handsome?"

"There is no story. We're friends. Jason's a good guy, but things are complicated enough right now. I can't think of anything more than friendship at the moment."

"Are you sure that's not just an excuse?" Lisa held up a hand to ward off Addison's denials. "Listen, I don't blame you for being nervous about starting something new. No one understands better than me." A flush crept across her cheeks. "But perhaps the key is moving on with the right person."

Addison arched her brows. "Ummm, is there something you aren't telling me?"

"Henry Rittenhouse and I started dating."

Addison knew Henry well because they'd gone to school together. He was a firefighter and volunteered tirelessly for church projects. His family was also wonderful and caring.

Addison couldn't keep the grin off her face. "When did this happen?"

Lisa's flush deepened. "We were on the volunteer committee for the Winter Fair and something just...clicked. He's kind and generous. Church-going. Incredibly sweet with my girls. It took me a while to get enough courage to take the first step. There was a lot of prayer involved. But I'm glad I did."

"I'm so happy for you. Henry's a great guy."

"He is. And so is Jason." Lisa lowered the towel. "Don't close your heart off to possibilities because you're scared, Addy. God has a plan for you. Don't tune him out."

It was excellent advice. She nodded. "I'll pray on it."

The door to the exercise room swung open. Rachel came in. Her dark hair was pulled back into a braid and she was dressed in comfortable gym clothes. She raced across the room and embraced Addison. "I was hoping to run into you here. How are you, Addy?"

"I'm okay, Rach. I appreciate the funny text messages you sent to lift my spirits." Addison pulled back and flashed her paralegal a smile. "And thanks again for offering to come and stay at my place last night. It was very sweet."

"It was the least I could do. The explosion yesterday was terrifying. I heard it all the way at the Dress Drive booth. It's a miracle no one was hurt." Rachel frowned. "People are saying it was some kind of gas leak, which struck me as strange considering someone had tried to kill you just 24 hours earlier."

"You're not the only one questioning the chain of events. The police are looking into it, but so far they can't connect the two incidents."

"Have they made any progress at all on the case?"

"It's complicated." Addison ran through everything that'd transpired since the bombing. "I'd assumed these attacks were connected to my job, but they may not be. Wendall could be behind them."

Rachel tossed her braid over her shoulder, a concerned look on her face. "Do you think Steven was telling the truth about not knowing where his father is?"

"I have no reason to doubt him." Addison pulled up the photograph of the SUV with the decal on her phone. "Kyle cleaned up the image of the SUV. Take another look. Have you seen it before? Or noticed anyone lingering around the office in the last few weeks?"

Rachel zoomed in on the decal. "No. This is distinctive. I would've remembered it. And I haven't seen anyone hanging around our offices lately." Her brow furrowed. "However, the floor above us is going through renovations and they have workers coming in and out all the time. I don't recognize most of them. Do you have a photograph of your father-in-law?"

Addison nodded and retrieved Wendall's mug shot that she'd saved on her phone. He had an angular face, beady eyes, and a full beard. "This was taken seven years ago. He's aged since then. Maybe shaved off his beard."

Rachel studied it for a few moments and then shook her head. "I don't know. He doesn't look familiar, but I can't be certain we haven't crossed paths and I simply don't remember. Can you send this to me? I'll give it to the security guards at our building and ask them to keep a look out. The SUV too."

"That's a great idea." Addison quickly forwarded both images.

Rachel's phone dinged. "Okay, I'll take care of that first thing in the morning. I'd better run or the trainer will be waiting for me. See you tomorrow in the office, Addy. Bye, Lisa."

Addison stopped her paralegal with a brush on her arm. "Wendall is the number-one suspect at the moment, but nothing is certain. He may not be behind these attacks. Be careful, Rach."

"I will be. Call if you need anything." Rachel gave a final wave and left.

Lisa shoved her towel back into her gym bag. "Let's get out of here. It's the end of the day for me, and I'm ready to get home to my girls."

"I don't blame you." Addison slung her gym bag over her shoulder. "It's getting late. Jason is probably outside waiting for me. He's been sticking close by since the attack at my house."

The two women meandered through the exercise equipment on the main floor. Addison waved goodbye to Rachel on the treadmill before stepping outside. The crisp air cooled her heated cheeks. She shrugged on her jacket, her gaze swinging toward Jason's vehicle. The handsome veteran was leaning against his SUV. He pushed off and started crossing the parking lot toward her, a wide smile on his face.

Addison's heart skipped a beat. Lisa hummed her approval and whispered something about chemistry.

Jason's gaze flickered to something behind Addison. A flash of panic crossed his face as a roar cut through the quiet afternoon. Addison spun in time to see a truck barreling down on her and Lisa.

Instinctively, Addison shoved her best friend out of the way. Lisa tumbled to the ground, rolling under a van. Addison ran to avoid the oncoming vehicle. The truck's engine roared as the driver punched the gas. He swerved.

Putting Addison squarely in his path.

SIXTEEN

Jason counted the distance to Addison in heartbeats, even as his mind absorbed details. One heartbeat. The truck was black with a front grill. Mud covered the license plate and sunlight glinted off the windshield, hiding the driver from view.

Two heartbeats. Jason's combat boots pounded against the pavement and the pins in his leg protested the impact. His gaze narrowed to Addison. The tilt of her body, the distance until she was free of the truck's path, the rate at which the vehicle was barreling down on her. Combat skills, buried but not forgotten, took over. They were as instinctive as breathing.

Three heartbeats. Jason hooked his arm around Addison's waist and then twisted away from the truck's path, lifting her off her feet. Momentum carried them into a parked sedan. Jason's body slammed into the unyielding metal door, pain shooting up his elbow, but his grip around Addison's waist remained firm.

The black truck whizzed past them. Tires squealing, it

shot out of the other side of the parking lot and sped toward the highway.

Jason sucked in a breath. White-hot agony vibrated along his side and arm, but he ignored it. His gaze swept the parking lot, searching for any other potential dangers, before settling on the woman in front of him. "Addison, are you hurt?"

She trembled in his arms and blinked, but then her gaze focused on his face. "I'm alive, thanks to you. Are you okay?"

"Fine." His elbow wasn't broken, just bruised. Jason had suffered enough injuries to know the difference. He held Addison at arm's length and scanned her, checking for injuries. Adrenaline could mask pain. But true to her word, she appeared unharmed.

Thank you, God. Even as he gave thanks, Jason mentally berated himself. The truck had approached from the left, and because of the damage to his hearing, Jason hadn't noticed the vehicle until it was closing in on Addison and Lisa.

"Lisa." Addison sucked in a breath. She pulled away from Jason and yelled, "Lisa!"

"I'm here. I'm okay." Lisa leaned heavily on the hood of a nearby van. Her face was contorted with obvious pain. "What just happened?"

"Someone tried to run over us. That's what." Addison raced to the other woman's side. "You're hurt."

"It's nothing serious. Bruised my hip and shoulder when I hit the ground." She grabbed Addison's hand. "If you hadn't pushed me—"

"Let's not think about that right now. The important thing is no one was seriously hurt."

Jason assessed Lisa's injuries. Her clothing was torn,

and although she was bleeding from a long scrape on her arm, the wound appeared superficial. "Did you bang your head on the ground, Lisa? Are you having any trouble breathing?"

"I'm fine." She pushed off the van, waving her hands dismissively. "Really. Don't fuss over me."

Rachel came running out of the gym with a cell phone in her hand. "I've called 911. They're sending police and an ambulance."

Lisa swayed. Jason wrapped an arm around her waist before she could topple over. Shock? Her eyes weren't dilated. She was probably crashing from the adrenaline.

"Lean on me, Lisa. Let's get you inside." Jason sent a pointed glance toward Addison. "Both of you."

It wasn't logical for the attacker to return, but running down two women in cold blood wasn't normal behavior. Jason wouldn't underestimate this man's determination or desperation. He'd tried to kill Addison three times in three days. And failed. That was liable to make him furious.

Please, God, give me the strength and wisdom to protect Addison until this criminal is caught.

The next few minutes were a flurry of activity. Police officers arrived. An ambulance took Lisa to the hospital to have her injuries examined. Rachel went with her.

Addison and Jason gave their witness statements separately. Forty minutes later, they were waiting in the gym's break room for Trevor. Jason watched through the full-length window as officers moved around the parking lot.

Addison appeared at his side, massaging a cold pack. She handed it to him. "Here, this should help your elbow."

"Thanks." He pressed the cold pack to his injury. "Any news on Lisa?"

"She's fine, just bumps and bruises. She's already been

discharged." Addison leaned against the window frame. "The guy in the truck swerved, Jason. He was purposefully trying to hit me."

"Yes, he was." Jason's jaw tightened, as those harrowing moments replayed in his mind. If he'd been a second later, Addison wouldn't be standing next to him now. It was terrifying to think about. He did his best to block out the emotions. They wouldn't help him find the man trying to kill her. "Did you get a look at the driver?"

"No. It all happened so fast." She frowned. "If Wendall is behind this, why did he switch vehicles? Why not use the SUV with the decal?"

"That's a good question." Jason lowered the ice pack from his elbow and stretched out his arm, testing the limits of the injury. "He could've stolen the truck. Or Wendall isn't behind this. Right now, I'm not sure we should take anyone off the suspect list."

Addison stepped forward, taking Jason's wrist in her hand. The warmth of her skin against his sent a jolt of awareness through him. His heart skipped several beats.

Addison's fingers brushed across the sleeve of his shirt. "Let me look at your elbow. If the swelling is bad, we should have it x-rayed."

He swallowed hard. "It's not broken. I've had worse."

She scoffed. "You would march into battle with a broken elbow and never complain."

She slid the sleeve up his arm. Jason considered pulling away, but his feet felt glued to the floor. Scars, similar to the one arcing across his cheek but thicker, crisscrossed along his arm. His stomach was a bundle of nerves, and he braced himself for Addison to pull back in disgust. Instead, she traced one scar gently with her finger. "From the IED?"

He nodded, not trusting his voice. Addison stepped

closer, maneuvering the sleeve carefully over his elbow. Her breath caressed his bare skin. The bundle of nerves in his stomach turned to molten heat.

She frowned, her gaze locked on his elbow. "The joint is swollen, but you're right. It doesn't appear broken. Just bruised."

Addison lifted her gaze to Jason's. This close the various flecks of gold and green buried in her gorgeous eyes were visible. They were mesmerizing. Her hair flowed loose around her shoulders. Addison's breath hitched and the air between them shimmered with intensity.

She was attracted to him. The realization hit Jason with the full force of a sledgehammer. He hadn't dared think... hadn't allowed himself to even consider...but it was there. In her eyes. In the subtle way she leaned closer. Addison's gaze dropped to his mouth, and Jason tilted toward her, unable to resist the yearning in her gaze.

Heavy footsteps echoed down the hall. Jason took one step back just as Trevor entered the break room. His expression was taut, his mouth grim. In one hand, he carried a small notepad. If he noticed the tension between Jason and Addison, the detective ignored it.

"Well, none of the witnesses could give me a description of the driver," Trevor said. "Everyone echoed what y'all told me. Black truck with a large front grill. I don't have to tell you that doesn't narrow things down much."

"Surveillance video?" Jason asked.

"The strip mall has a joint system for the parking lot and the stores. Yesterday, someone broke into the storage room and stole the equipment. At the time, I thought it was done by vandals looking for a quick buck. Given what happened this afternoon, however, that theory needs to be reassessed."

Addison stiffened. "Was the equipment stolen before or after the explosion at the abandoned store?"

Trevor paused. "After."

Jason edged closer to Addison, as if his presence alone could shield her. A break-in, a bombing, and now a hit-and-run. All of them had been planned. Whoever was behind this didn't care how he accomplished the task.

All that mattered was ending Addison's life.

"I've got every officer in the state looking for Wendall and the SUV with a decal." Trevor planted his hands on his leather duty belt. "We'll catch him. In the meantime, Addy, it's a good idea for you to leave town. Take a vacation, go to see your parents in Florida."

Addison shook her head. "I have obligations to my clients. The McCormick trial starts tomorrow."

"Postpone it. Given the circumstances, I'm sure the judge will agree."

"Absolutely not. Chloe deserves to have this case settled so she can move on with her life." Addison jutted up her chin. "Not to mention, we don't know who is behind these attacks. Can you guarantee I won't endanger my parents by going to their house?"

Trevor opened his mouth to answer and then snapped it shut. He blew out a breath. "No, I can't. You're right. Staying with your parents is a bad idea. But so is maintaining your routine. You come to boxing class every Monday."

Addison sank into a chair. "He's stalking me."

"I believe so. Your house, your office, the courthouse. They're all places you frequent regularly and it leaves you vulnerable to another attack."

"That may be, but I have a job to do. I can't walk away from it."

Trevor puffed out his cheeks. "You're being stubborn." His gaze shifted to Jason. "Help me out here."

Jason didn't like the request or the implication that went with it. His gaze settled on the detective. "Addison makes her own decisions."

She shot him a grateful glance, and Jason placed a hand on her shoulder. He understood Addison's commitment to her clients. Especially Chloe. Still, Trevor had a point. Addison needed a bodyguard until her attacker was caught. "If you're determined to see your cases through, Addy, then I'd like to help."

SEVENTEEN

Addison chopped fresh basil and oregano, letting the familiar scent soothe the last of her jagged nerves from the attack in the parking lot. On the stove, pasta sauce simmered. Another pot, filled with water, waited for the noodles. Garlic bread was baking in the oven. Comfort food. Something she could use right now. It'd been hours since the incident in the parking lot, but the fear lingered.

Shelby twined between her legs. Addison glanced down at the Siamese mix and smiled. "No, ma'am. Kitties don't eat spaghetti with meatballs."

The cat meowed in protest before plopping down to clean her paws. Addison tossed the herbs into the sauce and stirred. Jason, Nathan, and Kyle were coming over for dinner to discuss the case.

Addison was anxious to get to the bottom of things. Hopefully, Jason's friends had uncovered some information that would shed light on the identity of her stalker. The sooner he was caught, the better.

A knock came on the back door. Jason was visible through the glass. His hair was combed back from his face, but a five-o'clock shadow followed the powerful line of his jaw. He hadn't bothered with a jacket to ward off the cold, but had chosen a moss-green sweater instead. The fabric molded over his muscular shoulders.

Addison's heart skipped several beats. Every minute with the handsome Marine made it harder to ignore her growing feelings. She'd nearly kissed him in the break room this afternoon. If she was being honest, the pull toward Jason began long before the threats on her life. Their budding friendship over the last few months had laid the groundwork of trust and respect. She felt safe with him.

But was she taking advantage of his kindness? Since the break-in, Jason's life had been threatened twice—once with the bombing and then today he'd nearly been run over while rescuing her. But this wasn't his fight. Addison had an obligation to tell him so. Especially since he'd volunteered to be her bodyguard until the attacker was caught.

She fumbled with the alarm before opening the door. Connor bounded into the house, feet sliding over the tile. Jason tossed her a heartbreaking smile. "Hey."

"Hi." Addison shut the door against the wintry night. "Thanks for coming over a bit early. How's your elbow?"

"It's fine." Jason beelined for the stove and his mouth dropped open. "Aw, man, are these meatballs? Hurry, give me a plate before Nathan and Kyle get here."

She swatted at him playfully. "No way. You have to wait for everyone else."

Jason groaned, and they both laughed.

Addison opened a glass jar on the counter and removed a dog treat. She tossed it to Connor. He ate it in one bite and then settled on the carpet in front of the sink. Shelby drifted over to the dog and climbed on top of him, kneading his back. Connor sighed.

Addison raised a brow. "I can't tell if he likes Shelby or merely tolerates her."

"He likes her. Kyle's cat, Ms. Whiskers, approaches Connor and he dodges her. I've never seen them cuddle once." Jason leaned against the counter, making the sweater pull across his broad chest. "The guys will be here in about twenty minutes. What did you want to talk to me about?"

Nerves jangled in Addison's stomach, but she forced herself to meet his gaze. "Jason, I haven't been fair to you. You could've been killed today. Whoever this guy is, he's going to keep trying. I don't expect you to risk your life for me, and I should've said so after the bombing. If you want to walk away, I understand—"

"No." The word came out fast and harsh. Jason inhaled and then let it out slowly. "I want to see this through. Although it might be better to have Nathan or Kyle act as your bodyguard. I intended to speak to you about it tonight."

Addison swallowed down the rush of panic threatening to swell. Nathan and Kyle were good men, no doubt, but she trusted Jason implicitly. "I would prefer you."

"There are things you don't know about me, Addy." He tapped the left side of his head. "The hearing in this ear isn't perfect. The only reason I knew the truck was gunning for you was because I saw it. But I should've heard the engine before that. I didn't."

She hadn't known about his hearing loss, but it didn't change the way she felt. No one would protect her the way he had. "You saved my life, Jason, while risking your own. I couldn't ask for more."

He pushed away from the counter and took several steps across the kitchen. His back was rigid. "I have post traumatic stress disorder. Nightmares, the occasional flashback. Therapy has helped and I'm functional, but..." He turned to face her. "I've failed before. My fellow Marines died as a result. And that was when I was healthy and whole, not like I am now. You deserve the best, Addison."

The agony in his expression made Addison's heart weep. "You are the best."

He shook his head. "Please...don't give me platitudes."

"I'm not." Addison stepped forward until she was standing in front of him. "In the gym today, Lisa and I had a conversation, and she reminded me about something. God has a plan for me. I don't know why I'm being targeted or what will happen next, but I know one thing: I trust you, Jason. That's a huge thing for me. I've had a hard time trusting anyone—especially a man—since my divorce."

She gently reached up and touched his face, her finger trailing over the scar crisscrossing his cheek. "Being with you feels safe. There's no one else I want protecting me."

"Addy..."

Jason's hand came up to cup hers. The touch sent a wave of desire coursing through her. She was tired of fighting it. Tired of being afraid. For years, she'd avoided romance. But God had placed Jason in her path. Was it just to save her life? Or were these growing feelings for him a part of God's plan?

Addison stood on her tiptoes and brushed her lips against Jason's. The kiss was tender. Sweet. She pulled back, uncertainty sinking in as the repercussions of her bold move caught up to her.

Jason's hand tightened on hers. A subtle and yet powerful signal that she shouldn't pull away. Addison froze.

His gaze met hers. The passion buried in his stare stalled her breath. Jason tipped his head forward, capturing her mouth with his. Heat rocketed through her. She threaded her arms around his neck, dipping her hand into his thick hair. Addison couldn't get close enough to him. A whirlwind of emotion left no room for logic. She was lost, in a way she'd never experienced before. It should've terrified her, but it didn't. Jason would never hurt her.

The doorbell rang, barely registering in Addison's thoughts. Then it rang again. Jason broke off the kiss. He was breathing fast. Addison felt a secret rush of pleasure that the tough Marine was as rocked by their shared moment of passion as she was.

She glanced over her shoulder. "I should answer the door."

"I'll get it." Jason cleared his throat, but he didn't release her. Instead his thumb came up to brush against Addison's bottom lip. A rush of warmth coursed through her, but it was dampened by the confusion darkening his handsome features.

"Addy...kissing wasn't a good idea." Jason's gaze lifted to hers. "A relationship between us isn't possible, no matter how much I wish otherwise."

The doorbell chimed again. Jason made a disgruntled noise in the back of his throat. "Hold on," he yelled, before turning back to her. "I don't want to mess up our friendship."

"You didn't. I'm the one who kissed you."

Addison backed away. Why on earth had she been so impulsive? They'd never discussed the attraction between them, let alone dating or a future. And what did Jason mean when he said a relationship wasn't possible, no matter how much he wished otherwise?

She hugged her arms around herself. Questions rolled in her head in rapid-fire succession, but she couldn't formulate the words. "Get the door, Jason. We'll talk later."

"Are we okay?"

She nodded. The doorbell rang again. Jason slid past her and strolled to the door. Addison watched him go, her heart sinking. She didn't need this right now. More questions, more confusion. Not while someone was trying to kill her.

Had kissing Jason been a horrible mistake?

EIGHTEEN

Jason paused before opening Addison's front door. His heart was beating so hard, it was a wonder the organ didn't fail. The scent of Addison's perfume lingered on his clothes. It'd only been one kiss, but the ground had shifted beneath him.

The military had taught him discipline, to think with his head and not his emotions. Being with Addison...the woman got close to him and every one of his brain cells stopped operating. It was more than physical. There was an intimacy and closeness to their relationship Jason had never experienced before. As if he could tell her anything.

It was powerful. Heady.

Dangerous.

Jason needed to get it together. Kissing Addison had been a terrible mistake in judgment. It blurred the lines between them and risked ruining their friendship. Addison knew about his PTSD now, but she didn't understand the extent of it. Nightmares that made him scream and left him sweating and breathless. The depression that plagued him every year when the anniversary of the bombing arrived. A constant feeling of being on guard, alert for any danger.

The doorbell chimed again. As a precaution, Jason glanced through the peephole. Nathan and Kyle stood on the stoop. Jason grasped the handle and yanked open the door. A blast of cold air greeted him.

Nathan's thick finger was poised over the doorbell. He scowled. "Finally. What took you so long?"

Kyle's cowboy boots thumped on the tile floor as he crossed over the threshold. "Two more rings and we would've broken the door down." He jerked his head in Connor's direction. "The only reason we didn't was because the mutt had his nose pressed against the glass. I knew if something was wrong, Connor would be the first to tell us."

Jason caught the lettering on the side of the bakery box Kyle carried. Nelson's Diner. It was the restaurant they ate at on Wednesdays. "What's in the box?"

"It's not for you, Gonzalez. We figured Addison could use a treat after the week she's had." Kyle bellowed Addison's name before heading into the kitchen. "It smells amazing in here. What are we having for dinner? I hope it goes with apple pie."

Addison laughed. "Everything goes with apple pie."

Kyle scooped her up in a hug and then put the pie down on the counter. He opened the lid and Addison clapped her hands. The inaudible murmur of their voices filtered across the room.

Jason shut the front door. "I thought you guys were going to eat before you came over. Addy only has two boxes of pasta noodles. She's not used to feeding a group of men that eat like we do."

Nathan shrugged off his leather jacket. "How do you

think we got the apple pie? We ate at Nelson's. But that was hours ago and chasing down potential killers ain't easy. We worked up an appetite." He frowned, his sharp gaze assessing Jason. "You look upset."

"Someone is trying to kill Addison. That's not reason enough for you?"

"It is, but that doesn't explain why it took you so long to answer the door." Nathan tossed the jacket on the coat rack. He removed his cowboy hat and hung that up as well. "What's going on?"

He should've known Nathan would sense the tension. The former Green Beret had spent years rooting out terrorists and could read a room better than anyone. Jason shifted in his combat boots, trying to figure out how much was worth sharing with his good friend. Nathan had always been excellent at dispensing advice without coming across as judgmental.

But what was there to talk about? Yes, he'd shared a mind-blowing kiss with Addison, but it'd been a mistake. It wouldn't—couldn't—happen again. Talking to Nathan wouldn't change anything. The person Jason owed an explanation to was the gorgeous woman standing in the kitchen.

"Everything's fine. Or it will be fine once I fix it." Jason hoped so, anyway. It would be devastating to find out the kiss had completely ruined their friendship. He rubbed the back of his neck. Maybe it was a good idea to talk to Nathan, after all. "I told Addison about my PTSD."

"And?"

"She kissed me. And then I kissed her."

Nathan's mouth twitched. "This is a problem because..."

He glowered. "You know why it's a problem. Addison doesn't deserve to be saddled with my issues."

"Don't you think that's something Addison should decide?"

Jason opened his mouth and then snapped it closed. Nathan was right. Addison was a strong-willed and independent woman. She didn't need anyone—including Jason —making decisions for her.

He sighed. "I don't want to hurt her."

"So don't. Be honest with Addison about how you feel and what having PTSD means. Then give her the space and time to figure out what she wants." Nathan gave him a knowing look. "I hate to say this, Jason, but I think the person you're really protecting is yourself."

There was truth in his friend's observation. Jason was afraid of getting too close to Addison. What if she changed her mind about how she felt? Everything was moving so quickly, and emotions were heightened.

"I'll think about what you've said." Jason gestured toward the kitchen. "Come on, we'd better get in there before Kyle eats everything."

The two men made their way to the kitchen. Kyle was busy setting the table, while Addison stirred the pasta sauce on the stove. She shot them a wide smile. "Dinner is almost ready. I need five more minutes. Jason, do you mind getting Kyle and Nathan something to drink?"

"Not at all." He opened the fridge. "There's ice tea or soft drinks. What's your poison?"

Connor sprang from the kitchen mat in front of the sink and went to the back door. He growled, low and threatening.

Jason slammed the fridge shut, his hand automatically going to the concealed weapon along the small of his back.

"Kyle, stay here with Addison. Get her into a windowless room and call 911."

His friend sprang into action, hustling Addison out of the kitchen. Jason flipped off the kitchen lights as well as the porch ones before sliding up to the back door. The enemy they were up against would stop at nothing to eliminate Addison. Jason wouldn't put it past the man to shoot her from the tree line.

His gaze swept the backyard. "I don't see anything."

Nathan, gun in hand, stood in the home office. He parted the curtains. "Me either."

Connor growled again, clearly disagreeing with their assessment.

"Nathan, cover me." Jason didn't take his eyes off the tree line, even as he quickly punched in the code to disarm Addison's security system. "We need to capture him before the police arrive. Once he hears sirens, he'll bolt."

"Roger that." Jason didn't hear Nathan move back into the kitchen but sensed his presence behind him one moment before Nathan's hand landed on his back. "On your mark, Gonzalez."

"Connor, stay." Jason pointed to the living room. "Guard."

Connor would be useful for tracking the criminal, but the risk was too great. If the man had a gun and intended to use it, the German shepherd could be shot while crossing the yard. It was better to leave him here. If the attacker got past Nathan and Jason, he would have to go through both Connor and Kyle to get to Addison.

The dog backed away from the door, taking a position in the living room as ordered.

Jason popped the back door open. Frigid air swept over him as he darted for cover on the porch.

Gunshots erupted from the tree line. Bullets pelted the pillar, shooting bits of wood across the concrete stairs. The killer had no compunction about firing a weapon inside a neighborhood. Thank goodness Addison's house was at the end of the street, away from everyone else.

Jason's heart thundered, but the hand holding his weapon was steady. "Six o'clock."

"I see him." Nathan burst out of the house. More gunfire followed.

Jason didn't wait. He sprang from his position and raced across the wide expanse of the pitch-black yard. Every step, he half expected to feel the impact of a bullet slamming into him. It didn't happen. He burst past the tree line in time to hear the shooter running away.

Jason gave chase.

NINETEEN

Addison grabbed each side of her sweater and wrapped it around her midsection. Police officers tramped through her yard. There were more in the woods behind her house, their flashlight beams reflecting through the trees. Somewhere overhead an owl hooted. "I haven't seen or spoken to my father-in-law in over seven years."

Chief Walters glowered at the bullet holes in her porch pillar. "Well, he certainly seems to hate you enough to want you dead. All of this is over your husband?"

"Ex-husband. And yes, Wendall blames me for his son's death."

Movement from the tree line caught her attention. Jason stepped into the yard, moving toward the porch on sure strides. His combat boots were splattered with mud and a wayward leaf clung to his sweater. How close had he come to dying tonight?

Addison's chest tightened. She'd been hiding in the closet when the sound of gunshots rang out. The ten minutes following had been the worst of her life. She never wanted to go through anything like that again.

Trevor also stepped out of the woods. He followed Jason across the yard to the porch. The radio on his hip squawked, and he adjusted the volume.

"Anything?" Chief Walters asked, once the men were close enough.

"We located some bullet casings." Trevor stopped at the base of the porch stairs. "The shooter had a rifle. He got off a couple of extra shots at Jason in the woods before escaping. I'll have some officers canvass the area at first light. In the dark, it's too difficult."

Jason joined Addison on the porch. She reached for him instinctively, wrapping an arm around his waist. The fabric of his sweater was soft under her palm and the heat of his body drew her closer.

He reciprocated her touch. His hand was heavy on her hip. Solid. It made her feel feminine and delicate. Jason tucked her closer to his side before turning to the chief. "When the shooter fled, he left tire tracks on the dirt road."

"Good. I'll have the technicians make impressions of those tonight." The wind ruffled his thinning hair, revealing a bald spot. The chief smoothed a hand over the runaway strands. "Can you describe the vehicle he was driving?"

"An SUV of some kind. Dark colored. I can't swear it was the same SUV that passed outside Addison's house in the days prior to the break-in, but it's similar."

"What about the shooter?"

"Could be anyone." Frustration layered Jason's tone. "Average height and weight. He's in good shape but a terrible shot. He's also familiar with the woods behind Addison's house. He knew exactly how to navigate them. My guess is he used the same dirt road to escape on the night of the break-in."

"Probably right." Chief Walters frowned. "The park is

supposed to lock their gates at night, but they're lackadaisical about it. I'll talk to them in the morning. In the meantime, Addison, it would be a good idea for you to get out of town for a while."

"Trevor told me the same thing this afternoon, but I have obligations that can't be pushed aside. Besides, if my father-in-law is behind this, he'll follow me wherever I go."

The chief paused and then nodded. "All right then. I'll have patrol officers do more rounds outside your house. I've got more men searching for Wendall and the SUV. Chances are, he's hiding out somewhere here in town or close by."

"Chief, I have a friend who works with the Texas Rangers," Jason said. "You've spoken to him already. Ranger Grady West. I'm sure he'd be happy to lend a hand."

Chief Walters pursed his lips. "Appreciate the offer, but we've got this handled."

"With all due respect, sir, this is the second attack on Addison within a twenty-four hour period. This guy is escalating, and fast. I'm not trying to tell you how to do your job—"

"Then don't." He rocked back on his heels. "That reminds me. Friends of yours were asking questions about Michael McCormick, digging into his whereabouts on the night Ms. Foster was attacked and so forth."

Addison didn't have to ask how Chief Walters heard that piece of news. Michael must've gotten wind of their private investigation and called his friend.

"None of you are police officers," the chief continued. "You have no business investigating Michael or anyone else. If you persist, I'll be forced to arrest you for interfering with a police investigation."

Beside Chief Walters, Trevor pressed his lips together.

Addison had the vaguest impression he was pleased. Heat flooded her cheeks. Her life was being threatened, and they were more worried about appearances than finding the man responsible.

"I will continue to do everything within my power to protect Addison. That should put us on the same side, Chief, but if it doesn't..." Jason's tone was unyielding and unrepentant. "Then so be it."

Chief Walters narrowed his gaze. "We all want the same thing. Wendall Atkin behind bars where he belongs. Come on, Trevor. We have work to do." He nodded toward Addison. "Ma'am."

Trevor fell in step beside his boss. They joined some other officers in the yard. Addison watched them go, frustration burning her stomach. "Do you get the feeling we're being manipulated?"

"I'm not sure what to think." Jason tilted his head toward the house. "Let's go inside."

The kitchen was warm. Nathan and Kyle were sitting at the table, Connor at their feet. The pasta remained untouched on the stove.

Guilt swamped Addison. "Guys, what are you doing? Why didn't you eat?"

"Not without our hostess." Nathan rose, his bulky frame moving more gracefully than Addison would've thought possible. "Sit down, Addy. We can serve. What did the police say?"

Jason summarized what they'd discussed outside. Then he gently pushed Addison into a chair before she could form an objection. The scent of garlic and oregano mixed with tomatoes made her stomach grumble.

The three men bustled around the kitchen as though

they were used to working together. Within moments, a hot plate of food was set in front of Addison, along with a frosty glass of iced tea.

Nathan set two more plates piled high with pasta on the table and sat down. "Let's say grace and I'll tell you what I've learned about Wendall. Addison, will you do the honors?"

They joined hands. Addison bowed her head. "Thank you, Lord, for this meal. May it nourish our bodies. We also give thanks for Your safeguarding and protection. For friendship." She squeezed Jason's hand. "And for Your loving presence in our lives. Amen."

The men gave a chorus of amens in return.

Addison placed her napkin in her lap, then picked up her fork. She took a bite of pasta and sighed with pleasure as the flavors exploded on her tongue. Her three guests spent the next few minutes eating and complimenting her cooking. Despite the pressure of the situation and the stress of the last few hours, Addison relaxed.

Her gaze drifted over the guests at her table. Nathan and Kyle were handsome men in their own right. Considerate. Brave. Any woman in her right mind would jump at the chance to be in a relationship with either of them. But Addison only felt friendly affection for the two men.

She peeked at Jason and her pulse jumped. Everything about him drew her in. Their conversation from earlier replayed in her mind. *A relationship between us isn't possible, no matter how much I wish otherwise.* Knowing what she did about him, it sounded like Jason was trying to protect her. The question was: from what?

She didn't know. But Addison had every intention of finding out.

Jason wiped his mouth with a napkin. "Okay, Nathan, spill it. What did you learn about Wendall Atkin?"

"This won't come as a surprise, but Wendall is bad news." Nathan reached for the salad bowl. "I checked into the murder case he went to prison for. Wendall broke into the man's house and beat him to death."

Jason's hand tightened on his fork. "That's similar to the initial attack on Addison."

"I had the same thought. Wendall was staying at a pay-as-you-go motel following his release from prison, but disappeared about a month ago. I spoke to several family members. No one has seen or heard from Wendall in weeks. However, they confirmed what Wendall's son, Steven, told you. The SUV with the decal looks like Wendall's vehicle. He kept it at his sister's house while he was in prison."

"Is she in contact with him now?" Jason asked.

"No. She recommended I speak to Steven. Apparently, he was visiting Wendall in prison."

Addison stilled, fork halfway to her mouth. "Steven swore he hadn't been in contact with his dad for years."

"He lied to you. Wendall's sister was adamant Steven and his dad were in constant communication. Wendall even worked for Steven's construction company for a bit."

Kyle twirled pasta around on his fork. "Is Steven a part of this? Wendall wants revenge for his son's death. Grief has a funny way of affecting people. Maybe time gave Steven an opportunity to think about joining his father's crusade."

"I have a hard time believing that." Addison pushed away her plate. She'd lost her appetite. "Steven was the only family member to stand by me when I divorced Greg. And we've been in contact with each other all this time. If Steven wanted revenge, he could've attacked me a long time ago."

The three men didn't look convinced. She couldn't blame them.

Steven *had* lied.

But why?

TWENTY

The next morning, Addison smeared on lip gloss. Her black turtleneck dress covered the faded bruises along her throat. Paired with heels, a red suit jacket, and minimal jewelry, the outfit conveyed control and power. Chloe McCormick's divorce hearing was set for this afternoon. Facing Michael and his expensive attorneys required confidence.

She flipped off the bathroom light, stuck her cell phone into the pocket of her suit jacket, and headed for the kitchen. Shelby was lying smack in the center of the island. Addison planted her hands on her hips. "You naughty cat, you know you're not supposed to be up there."

Shelby blinked her feline eyes, but otherwise refused to move. Addison glanced down at her black dress and winced. "Picking you up isn't an option. I can't go to work covered in cat hair."

Shooing her from the counter wasn't a viable choice either. Shelby had been abused as a kitten, which is how she ended up at the shelter. Addison took great care to be gentle with her cat, and they'd built a lovely bond.

She poured a cup of coffee, wishing she could inject the

caffeine straight into her veins. Sleep had been elusive last night. Trevor's warning words haunted her. The courthouse was a place she frequented. Would her attacker make another attempt on her life there? It was a terrifying thought, but she wouldn't give in to the fear. She'd done that in her marriage with her abusive husband, and it'd cost Addison a piece of herself. Never again.

Movement outside the window caught her attention. Jason was standing in the middle of her yard, Connor by his side. Both of them had their gazes locked on the tree line. Addison pulled another cup from the cabinet and filled it to the brim. She left the brew undoctored. Jason preferred it black.

Stepping onto the porch, Addison drew in a deep breath. The air was scented with pine and dew-soaked grass.

Connor bounded over, tail wagging. Addison couldn't pet him since her hands were full. She greeted him with a smile. "Hey, buddy, how are you this morning? Is it safe for me to come outside?"

"It is." Jason climbed the steps. "Kyle is patrolling the woods. It's been quiet all night."

Butterflies flitted in Addison's stomach, growing stronger the closer Jason came. He wore professional slacks and a burgundy button-down shirt. The color brought out his olive skin and dark eyes. He'd trimmed the permanent five o'clock shadow on his jaw as well.

"Morning." Jason gestured to the coffee mugs in her hand. "Are one of those for me or are you double fisting it this morning?"

Addison blinked, belatedly realizing she'd been standing there like a dunce staring at him. Heat rose in her cheeks and she thrust the undoctored coffee in his direction. "Morning. You look nice."

"Thanks. Since I'm going to work with you today, I wanted to make sure I fit in." He sipped the dark brew, making a noise of appreciation. "You make the best coffee. What time did you want to leave this morning?"

"Around ten. I'll go to the office first and then I'm scheduled to meet Chloe at the courthouse an hour before the trial starts." Addison crossed to the porch swing and took a seat. She sipped her coffee, gathering her thoughts. She and Jason were going to be spending the day together. Maybe it was wiser to let sleeping dogs lie, as the saying went, but it felt strange to ignore the sizzling attraction between them. Especially given the kiss they'd shared.

"Jason, I was hoping we could talk about what happened between us. Last night, when you said that we could never have a relationship, even though you wished it could be otherwise..." She lifted her gaze to meet his. "What did you mean by that?"

Jason sighed and joined her on the porch swing. He gently pushed them back and forth. "It's complicated. In order for you to understand, I have to tell you the whole story about what happened to me in Afghanistan."

"I want to hear it." She bit her lip. "But if you'd rather not talk about it now, that's okay. I didn't realize—"

"No, I'm glad you asked. I've been thinking about how to bring it up for most of the morning."

Addison reached across and took his hand. She interlocked their fingers. "Then tell me."

"In Afghanistan, Connor and I were clearing the outside of a building with several other members of my team. Something caught Marcus's eye..." He glanced at her. "You remember I told you about Marcus?"

She nodded, recalling the beautiful painting in his house of the little girl and the soldier. Maddy was the child's name. She was Jason's goddaughter. "Marcus is Maddy's biological father. The one she'd never met."

"Yes. Anyway, something caught his eye. I never learned what. Marcus and the others ran down the street." His gaze drifted off, seeing something Addison couldn't. "A car bomb detonated. All of them were killed. Connor and I were the only ones to survive."

The pain in Jason's voice crushed her. Addison bit the inside of her cheek to keep her eyes from filling with tears. "I can't imagine what that must've been like for you."

"Life-altering. The bombing changed me, Addy. I'm not...normal. I have nightmares so real, I wake up screaming. I'm plagued with anxiety. Therapy has helped me control it, but the occasional flashback will catch me off guard."

Addison kept quiet, sensing that he had more to say. The chain securing the porch swing creaked with the back-and-forth movements.

"Each year, when the anniversary of the bombing comes around, I check out from life. I head to a cabin in the woods and live there for two weeks." Connor nudged his master, as if sensing his emotions, and Jason petted him. "It's my way of coping. Or maybe grieving. I don't know."

She squeezed his hand. "Sometimes we need to get away from everything in order to hear God better. Does going to the cabin help?"

"Help is relative. It doesn't make the loss or the memories go away, but you're right, it does give me time to pray and think." He turned to face her. "The thing is, Addy, my PTSD isn't a short-term thing. I may have it the rest of my life. You deserve to know that."

She studied his face, the hard lines and sharp edges. The scars coursing down his cheek. "Are you afraid I'll see you differently?"

"Yes, but it's more than that." He blew out a long breath. "Here's the deal. A lot of my military friends had wives or girlfriends when they went overseas. Then they came back, changed men. It was hard on their loved ones. Living with PTSD full-time is rough on everyone. Some of my buddies...their relationships didn't survive."

Addison let his words sink in and understanding dawned. He was scared. Afraid she would change her mind after starting a relationship with him.

A swell of emotions battled inside her. She took a moment to gather her thoughts. It was important to get this right. "Jason—"

Her cell phone trilled. Addison wanted to ignore it so they could continue the conversation, but the threats against her had to take precedence. It could be Trevor or Chief Walters calling with an update. Or even Chloe, nervous about the trial this afternoon.

"I'm sorry." She removed the phone from her suit jacket, glancing at the screen. "It's Rachel. I should answer because this could be about the trial." Addison raised a finger. "But the conversation between us isn't over, just postponed."

Jason hesitated and then nodded.

Addison answered. "Hey, Rach, everything okay? Have you had a problem reaching Chloe this morning?"

"No, no. Chloe's fine. She's ready for court this afternoon." Rachel took a deep breath. "Actually, I'm calling about you. More specifically, the threats against you."

Addison punched the speaker button on her phone.

121

"Rachel, just so you know, I'm here with Jason. He can hear you. Go ahead."

"I asked building security guards about Wendall this morning like we discussed," Rachel said. "I showed them his picture. No one recognized him, but several said they'd noticed a man hanging around the building lately. We have cameras so I asked for the footage. Addison, you need to see it."

Her voice was grave, and it ramped up Addison's apprehension. Her phone dinged with an incoming message. She scrolled to it and started the video, ignoring the way her fingers trembled.

A man came on screen, pacing the public sidewalk across the street from her office building. He wore jeans and a polo shirt. A ball cap covered his head. The man faced away from the camera initially, but something about his stride was familiar as he ambled to the corner. Then he turned, and the camera caught his face.

Addison gasped. "It's Steven Atkin."

TWENTY-ONE

Atkin Construction was in a two-story professional building close to Addison's office. Jason pulled into the parking lot and killed the engine. "Are you sure about this?"

Addison's lips flattened into a hard line. "The video looks bad, but I can't believe Steven is behind the threats against me. There has to be a reasonable explanation."

Jason was tempted to argue with her, but she'd been through the wringer this week. Steven was Addison's friend. He'd supported her through one of the hardest times of her life—her divorce. Jason couldn't blame her for defending the man. "Okay then. Stay in the vehicle. I'll come around."

He got out of his truck. The parking lot was devoid of people, but nerves jittered his insides. They were working against a clock. Jason could feel it. The shooting last night hadn't been as well planned as the previous attacks. It'd been more desperate. Things were escalating, and it was only a matter of time before the criminal made his next move.

Jason opened the passenger-side door, offering his hand to help Addison down. Her fingers were delicate, the nails painted a pale lavender. A cross bracelet was tangled with her watch. He gently separated them.

Addison licked her lips. "Thanks."

Her voice was breathy, as if his touch upended her. Jason's gaze dropped to her luscious mouth. He was in serious trouble. He'd foolishly thought their conversation this morning would act as a dose of cold water on the attraction between them, but it hadn't.

It took every ounce of his willpower not to kiss her. Jason released her hand and cleared his throat. "Come on. Let's get this done."

They started across the parking lot toward the building. Sunlight glinted off the front door as it opened. Steven Atkin strolled out. His dark hair was slicked back from his face and a pair of sunglasses was tucked in the collar of his polo shirt under a lightweight jacket. In one hand, he carried a cardboard tube that probably contained architectural plans. His cell phone was in the other hand. His thumb flew over the screen, as if he was sending a text message.

"Hi, Steven." Addison waved.

Steven's head jerked up. A flash of something crossed his features but disappeared so quickly Jason almost thought he'd imagined it. The knot in his stomach tightened. Steven was the same height and weight as the shooter.

Was Steven working with his dad? Or worse, was he responsible for all the attacks against Addison?

Steven clicked his phone shut and plastered on a smile a bit too forced to be real before setting a path to intercept them. "Addison, hey. I didn't know you were coming. You should have texted me. I'm just on my way out to meet with a client."

"We need to talk, Steven, and it can't wait." She pointed to a picnic table under a nearby tree. "Let's sit over there."

For a moment, Jason thought Steven was going to refuse, but then his shoulders dropped and he strolled toward the table with long strides. Birds fluttered overhead in the oak tree. The thick branches cast a long shadow and dried leaves littered the grass. Jason was careful to position himself between Addison and Steven. The risk to her safety might be minimal, but it wasn't zero. He wouldn't take any chances.

"Okay." Steven crossed his arms over his chest and the fabric of his jacket rustled. "What's this about?"

Addison removed her cell phone from the pocket of her coat and pulled up the surveillance video. She flipped the phone around so Steven could view the screen. "You've been watching the outside of my workplace, and I want to know why."

Steven's complexion paled. "I can explain."

"Then I would recommend you start talking." Jason pinned him with a hard look. "We know you've been in contact with your dad. Family members told us you visited Wendall frequently in prison. This video was taken before there were any attempts on Addison's life. From where I'm standing, it looks like you had knowledge of Wendall's intentions. Or worse, you're helping."

"No." Steven stiffened. "I would never hurt Addison. Never."

He was so adamant, Jason was tempted to believe him. But Steven had lied to them in the past and done a convincing job of it. He couldn't be trusted.

Steven stumbled back and sagged against the edge of the picnic table. His hands gripped the wood hard enough to turn his knuckles white. "I was worried. That's why I've been watching your office."

Addison's lips flattened into a thin line. "So you knew my life was in danger and you didn't say a word to me?"

"No, I didn't know anything for sure. Let me explain." He took a deep breath. "After he went to prison, Wendall wrote me letters. He apologized for things that had happened during my childhood and begged me to visit him. Over time, we built a relationship. I thought he was a changed man."

"He tricked you."

Steven ran a hand through his thick hair. "Worse. He was using me."

"What does that mean?" Jason asked.

"After Wendall was released from prison, he started dropping comments." Steven swallowed hard. "They were easy to ignore in the beginning, but eventually, it became clear Wendall was attempting to manipulate my feelings toward Addison."

Addison bit her lip. "He wanted you to hate me."

Steven nodded. "It's hard to describe how things progressed. Wendall didn't wake up one day and insist Greg's death was your fault. If he had, it would've been easy to walk away from him. It was more subtle than that. And by then, my dad and I had a close bond. I...I didn't want to lose the relationship we'd built, so I ignored what was happening right in front of my face." He lifted his gaze to hers. "I'm sorry, Addy. I've made a lot of mistakes."

She let out a long breath and her shoulders dropped. "I know what that's like, Steven. I was married to Greg. I know exactly how complicated relationships can get, especially when manipulation and abuse are involved."

Jason rocked back on his heels. Addison might be

willing to overlook Steven's cowardly actions, but he wasn't. The man knew his father held ill will toward Addison and said nothing to warn her. Nor was he upfront when they spoke to him a few days ago.

"If you knew Wendall was a threat to Addison, why didn't you turn him into the police?" he asked.

"You don't understand. Wendall didn't want to kill Addison." Steven's expression hardened. "He wanted me to."

Addison's mouth dropped open. "What?"

"Wendall hated prison. He never wanted to go back. My dad hoped to manipulate me into doing his dirty work for him. I refused, and we had a fight. After that, Wendall disappeared and I haven't seen him since."

"When was this?"

"About a month ago." He gestured toward her phone. "That's why I was watching the outside of your office. I didn't think Wendall would try anything on his own, but I couldn't be certain. Again, I'm sorry, Addy. I should've been upfront with you."

She tilted her head, a crease forming between her brows. "Why weren't you?"

"I was ashamed." A flush crept across Steven's face and his gaze skittered away from hers. "Wendall fooled me. I thought he wanted a relationship with me, but all he actually cared about was hurting you."

Jason's gaze narrowed. He wasn't completely buying Steven's act. Something about this wasn't ringing true. Nor was it logical. Steven claimed to care about Addison, but he did nothing to warn her. Why?

Steven checked his watch and stood. "I've got to go. My client is waiting." He paused. "Addy, there's one more thing. I'm not sure my dad is the one after you now. As much as

127

Wendall hates you, he despises prison more. Killing you is risky. That's why he wanted me to do it."

Jason locked eyes with Steven. "Do you know where Wendall is?"

"No." He picked up the cardboard tube from the table. "If he contacts me, I'll let you know. But he won't. Wendall has no use for me now." Steven nodded toward Addison. "Stay safe."

He strolled across the parking lot and got into a silver pickup. Steven barely tapped the brakes as he peeled out of the parking lot.

Uneasiness plagued Jason. He rubbed the back of his neck. "I hate to say this, Addison, but Steven knows more than he's saying. He's protecting Wendall. I think he knows exactly where his father is."

She sighed. "So do I."

TWENTY-TWO

The family courthouse entrance was a bustle of activity as people moved in and out of the main doors. Addison checked her watch for what seemed like the zillionth time. Her heels clicked against the marble floor as she paced in front of the long windows overlooking the sidewalk. There was no sign of Chloe.

"I don't understand." Addison's fingers tightened on her briefcase. "Where is she?"

Jason placed his hands on her shoulders. "The trial doesn't start for another forty-five minutes. Even people who aren't normally late hit a glitch every once in a while. Is this genuine worry or is this stress talking?"

He was right to ask. A constant fear plagued her every move. What would Wendall do next? The conversation with Steven hadn't helped. He'd betrayed her, lied to her. It was painful to realize her friendship with him was false.

She'd shoved all of her problems to the back of her mind and focused on preparing for the upcoming trial, but it hadn't been easy. Now, standing around waiting for Chloe to arrive brought all of her emotions to the forefront.

Addison sucked in a breath and then let it out slowly. Her heart rate dropped and some of the tension in her muscles left. "You're right. It's been a rough day."

The corner of his mouth quirked. "Addy, it's been a hard *five* days. I've seen soldiers break under this kind of pressure. It's a wonder you're still standing, let alone walking into a courtroom to fight for your client."

"I won't be much good to Chloe if I'm a neurotic mess."

She took another deep breath and sent up a silent prayer for strength. She had to get through this trial. After that, Addison could lock herself in her house until the police got enough evidence to arrest Wendall. Or Steven. Or both.

A long strand of people waited to get through security. Addison scanned the lines but didn't see Chloe. She moved back to the window. "I offered to send Kyle to pick Chloe up, but she refused. She didn't want to be in a car with a strange man. Maybe I should've sent Rachel instead."

"Are you worried Chloe will get cold feet?"

"A bit. She called me on Friday night, stressed about seeing Michael in court. It's difficult to face your attacker, especially when it's your husband or someone you love. Rachel spoke with Chloe this morning and is certain she'll show, but..." Addison rubbed her forehead. Another headache was brewing. They'd been constant today, a side effect of stress. "Things can change. I'm going to call her myself. It'll make me feel better."

Addison pulled out her cell phone and dialed Chloe's number. It rang and then went to voice mail. Maybe she was driving and couldn't answer the phone. Addison sent her a text and then called Rachel.

Her paralegal answered on the first ring, slightly out of breath. "I'm two blocks away from the courthouse."

"Chloe isn't here yet. I've tried calling her, but she's not answering. How was she when you spoke to her this morning?"

"Ready to get the trial over with. I don't understand... Chloe is never late to anything, and I specifically told her to meet you at the courthouse entrance at noon sharp." Rachel's worried tone matched Addison's own instincts. "I'll call Chloe's mom. Maybe there was an issue with the baby."

Rachel hung up. Addison called Chloe's number again. The phone rang and, again, went to voice mail. "Jason, I can't explain it, but something is wrong."

He didn't tell her she was overreacting. Instead, he pulled out his own phone. "I'll call Kyle. Maybe he's close by and can check on her."

Addison sent another text to Chloe, half listening to Jason's side of the conversation with Kyle. His buddy wasn't close from what she could gather. Jason hung up and called another number, probably Nathan.

Frustration fueled Addison's steps as she strolled to the windows again. Her gaze swept over the outside stairs, as well as up and down the block. Still no sign of Chloe.

The inexplicable sensation of being watched prickled the back of Addison's neck. She turned.

Michael McCormick, flanked by his attorneys, had entered the courthouse. He was standing in the security line, wearing a designer business suit and shoes that cost more than Addison's yearly food bill. His attorney was saying something, but Michael appeared to be ignoring him. His focus was solely on Addison.

Their gazes met. Michael smirked, a triumphant look in his eyes.

Addison's body went ice cold.

Jason appeared by her side. His attention was drawn to Michael, across the room. Whatever he saw in the other man's expression put the former Marine into action. Jason's hand landed on the small of Addison's back as he propelled her toward the double set of doors. "Let's go."

She needed no further encouragement. Addison broke into a run as they hit the stairs, her sole focus on finding Chloe.

Rachel intercepted them. "Chloe dropped the baby off with her mom more than an hour ago. She was going to her apartment to finish getting ready and then heading to court."

That gave them a starting point. Addison shoved her briefcase at her paralegal before hurrying down the last of the stairs. "Stall the judge any way you can."

She didn't bother to wait for Rachel's response. Grabbing Jason's hand, Addison raced to the parking garage and his vehicle.

Please, Lord. Please don't let us be too late.

Jason raced through every light of downtown Austin. In the passenger seat, Addison clutched the handle above the door, whispered prayers falling from her lips. She'd tried calling Chloe half a dozen more times. Each attempt went to voice mail.

Something was definitely wrong.

Tires squealing, Jason turned into Chloe's apartment complex. He braked, bringing the truck to a stop along the fire lane. Parking there was illegal, but urgency fueled his movements along with the memory of Michael's smirk.

Addison jumped from her seat and raced for the rickety

staircase. Jason followed, catching up to her on the landing. The metal stairs swayed from the force of their steps. On the third floor, Jason grabbed Addison's arm, pulling her to a stop. "Get behind me."

She nodded. Jason assessed the landing and entrance to Chloe's apartment. Nothing seemed disturbed. The mat was flush against the door and there were no scratches around the lock that would indicate a break-in. There was only one other apartment on the landing, the entrance opposite Chloe's. Based on the bare rooms visible through uncurtained windows, the unit was empty.

Jason knocked. "Chloe, it's Addison and Jason. Are you there?"

No one answered. Jason dropped his hand to the handle and twisted. The door popped open.

Addison sucked in a breath. She leaned in closer to him and whispered, "Chloe would never leave her home unlocked."

He nodded sharply. He remembered the last time they'd visited, Chloe had used the chain and deadbolt. Jason removed his gun from the holster concealed under his jacket. He kept the weapon's muzzle pointed at the ground as he used his foot to push the door open wider. "Chloe, it's Jason and Addison. Are you here?"

Silence.

The living room and kitchen appeared undisturbed. A blanket was folded across the back of the futon while toys poured from a bucket on the floor. It smelled like coffee and baby powder. Nothing was amiss and yet the hair on the back of Jason's neck rose. His gut was never wrong, and he wouldn't ignore it now.

"Stay behind me," Jason whispered.

Addison nodded.

He stepped farther into the apartment, his boots sinking into the stained carpet. Addison followed his movements, her hand wrapped around the back of his belt. The curtains in Chloe's apartment were closed, blocking most of the natural light.

The hallway leading to the bathroom and master bedroom was on the left. Jason traversed the narrow path. The bathroom door was open. A towel rested on the side of the bathtub. Water droplets lingered in the sink.

Chloe had been here recently. Where was she now?

The only possibility left in the apartment was the bedroom. Jason's heart raced as dread settled into his bones. No sound emanated from behind the cracked-open door. He feared what they would find once they crossed the threshold.

"Chloe, are you here? It's Jason and Addison."

He hoped against hope the young woman was merely sleeping. Jason once again used his foot to ease the door open. A single bed covered in a quilt came into view. The nightstand next to it held a lamp, a book, and a cell phone charger. The closet door, located on the other side of the bedroom, was shut tight. Dust motes danced in the light coming from a single window. Nothing appeared disturbed or out of place.

Jason quickly crossed the room and opened the closet door. A light flickered on, revealing a suitcase, a row of shoes, and an assortment of women's clothing. Several shelves held baby items.

Chloe wasn't here.

Addison let out a breath and released the back of Jason's belt. She rubbed her fingers, as if they were stiff. "I don't understand. Where is she? Chloe would never leave the door to her house unlocked, even if she was in a hurry. Safety is very important—"

A whoosh came from the living room. Jason's heart stuttered and then took off as a familiar sound reached his ears.

Fire.

He grabbed Addison's hand and ran into the hallway. Smoke assaulted his senses. The entire main living area was ablaze. The flames transfixed him, transporting him back to Afghanistan and the bombing.

Jason's scars burned, the pain unreasonable and unrelenting. He screamed. His knees hit the floor as he collapsed to the ground.

TWENTY-THREE

The fire was terrifying, but the screams coming from Jason were more so. He was having a flashback. Addison dropped to her knees beside him, shaking his shoulder, shouting to be heard over the smoke detector's warning siren. "Jason."

He ignored her, lost in the memory and trapped in his mind. Heat from the flames poured over Addison. The entire living room was on fire, including the area in front of the entrance. They were trapped in the apartment.

The scent of gasoline assaulted her nose, erasing any doubt that this was a planned attack on her. Or Chloe. They still didn't know where her client was.

"Jason."

She shook his shoulder more forcefully this time. Again he didn't respond except to howl in pain. The sound sank into her with fierce claws. She'd never heard anything like it. Somewhere inside, her heart was breaking for Jason and what he'd been through. What he was suffering from, even now. But there was no time to waste. The flames were growing by the second and the smoke was getting thicker. They couldn't stay put.

Addison ran into the bathroom and grabbed the towel hanging on the bathtub. She soaked the fabric with water. A hasty search of the bathroom yielded two more towels. She wet those as well before going back into the hall.

Jason was still on the ground, clutching his shoulder. His eyes were staring some place she couldn't see. His face was contorted with pain and grief. Reliving the death of his fellow Marines? That's what it looked like.

She touched his face with the wet towel, hoping it would shock him back into the present. "Jason, it's Addison. You need to get up. Now."

No response. The flames were hotter, and the smoke burned Addison's lungs. She could try dragging Jason but doubted she had the upper body strength. Her mind raced as she tried to remember tips about suffering from PTSD. She'd had her own bouts with it after her divorce. Most of the advice was self-directed. Take deep breaths, remind yourself that you're safe, focus on the five senses in the surrounding space.

None of that was helpful at the moment.

Addison's hand tightened around the wet towel. Her father was a fan of military movies, the kind with drill sergeants barking out orders. If Addison couldn't reach Jason by being herself, maybe she could by being someone else.

"Gonzalez, snap out of it." Addison yelled the commands. "Get to your feet, Marine. Move it!"

Jason blinked. His eyes landed on her face, and she recognized the minute he actually returned to the present. The haze in his gaze cleared.

She tugged on his arm. "Let's go."

He shot to his feet, grabbed her hand, and pulled her into the master bedroom. Addison slammed the door behind them. The buzzing from the apartment's smoke alarm faded. She shoved the wet towels into the cracks at the bottom and top of the door. It wasn't much against the thick smoke, but it was better than nothing.

Glass shattered. She turned in time to see Jason pull his hand—covered in his jacket—back from the window. He knocked out the rest of the shards before leaning out.

Addison raced to his side. Fresh air poured into the room and she drew it into her lungs. "Is there a fire escape?"

"No." Jason screamed for help, his voice weakened by the smoke inhalation.

Addison joined his efforts. No one appeared in the alley. The location was off the main road, and most of the people living in the apartments were at work. Smoke thickened in the bedroom, and despite the fresh air, Addison started coughing. The heat from the fire increased the room temperature at an alarming rate.

Would they die from the smoke? Or from the flames?

Her gaze darted over the bedroom. "Maybe Chloe has a fire ladder."

"She doesn't. I already checked the closet and under the bed." Jason turned to face her. "Addy, we have to walk to the next apartment."

"Walk?" Addison leaned on the windowsill as far as she dared. A small, decorative ledge jutted out from the side of the building. Her heart dropped to her feet before rising up to lodge in her throat. She ripped her hand from Jason's. "No. No. No. I can't."

"We don't have a choice."

Panic welled as Addison's fear of heights sent her head spinning. She could barely drive over multi-lane bridges. Zip-lining was out of the question. So was rock climbing. Her feet had to be firmly planted on the ground.

"I'm sure someone has called the fire department. We can wait."

Jason grabbed her shoulders. "No, we can't. The fire is about to eat its way through the door."

The crackle of the flames grew louder as the wooden bedroom door groaned and popped. Her knees weakened as the truth about their precarious situation hit home. Smoke cast a haze over the room. Sweat dripped down her back.

"I'm going to be with you, Addy. Every step. Holding your hand." Jason dipped his head, forcing Addison to meet his gaze. "You're the strongest woman I've ever met. You can do this."

Her insides quivered. She had to do this. If she refused, Jason would stay, too, putting his own life at risk. Scaling the ledge to the next apartment's window was their only chance of survival.

She gave a sharp nod of consent, not trusting her voice.

Jason pulled her back to the window. "I'll go first."

Addison held her breath as Jason put one leg out the window and then the other. Bile rose in the back of her throat and her body shook. She clenched her jaw to keep her teeth from rattling.

He eased across the ledge with grace before holding out a hand to her. "Okay, now you."

It took everything inside Addison to reach across the distance and place her hand in Jason's. "Lord, please give us strength. And steady steps."

"Give us Your protection," Jason said, taking up the prayer. He gently squeezed Addison's hand. "We can do all things with Your help."

Yes, they could do all things with the Lord's help. Addison closed her eyes, gathering every ounce of courage within her. She wasn't alone. She had the Lord. And Jason.

She could do this. She *would* do this.

Addison opened her eyes with a snap. She grabbed the window's edge with trembling fingers and kicked off her high heels before swinging one leg over the edge. The concrete ledge was rough under her bare skin. Cold air cooled the sweat beaded on her brow and she shivered.

"Now, the other foot, Addy." Jason kept his gaze locked on her. "You can do it."

A fierce whoosh came from inside the apartment as the bedroom door gave way. Smoke and flames poured into the room. Addison quickly swung her other leg out. The fire singed her hair and intense heat burned her back.

Jason tugged on her hand. "Slide, Addy."

She said another prayer, gripping Jason's hand hard enough it was any wonder his bones didn't snap, and eked to the side. The fabric of her jacket scraped against the brick. Wind ruffled her hair. She gripped the wall with her other hand, her nails searching for some kind of traction, and looked down.

The ground swam before her eyes. She imagined her body crashing into the cement and shattering into a thousand pieces. Her heart thundered against her rib cage. She couldn't breathe.

"Look at me," Jason ordered.

Her gaze snapped to his. The sunlight brightened the color of his eyes to a stunning shade of brown, reminiscent of melted chocolate. Some of Addison's fear ebbed. She sucked in a deep breath and let it steady her nerves.

"Keep moving, Addison. Sliding toward me. That's it."

Her feet scraped against the concrete ledge. "If I make it to the other window, I'm buying an apple pie from Nelson's Diner every week for the next two months."

His mouth quirked. "You liked it that much, huh?"

"Are you kidding? It's the best pie I've ever had." Focusing on sweets and Jason was a lot better than thinking about how easy it would be to plunge to her death with one wrong move.

Jason kept the conversation going as they traversed the distance to the next window. He punched it with his fist. The sound of shattering glass had never been so sweet. Addison's knees wanted to go weak with relief. She forced them to hold strong.

"Home stretch, Addy. You're doing great." Jason climbed in through the opening, his hand still holding hers. "Keep coming this way."

She refused to look down. Keeping herself distracted was the key. "Just in case you get any bright ideas, I'm not skydiving with you after this." She shifted her body to enter the window. "Conquering your fears is overrated—"

Her foot slipped off the ledge.

TWENTY-FOUR

Everything happened in slow motion.

One moment Addison was in front of him. The next, her foot slipped off the ledge. Jason's body pitched forward as his waist pressed against the hard edge of the windowsill. His hand clutched Addison's. Her body jerked to a stop along the side of the building and pain erupted along his shoulder.

One hand. It was the only thing keeping Addison from plummeting into the unforgiving concrete below.

She screamed. Sheer terror and panic was etched across every curve of her face. Her feet dangled and Addison instinctively flailed. Every movement dragged Jason further out of the window and loosened his precarious grip on her hand.

"Stop." His tone was sharp and unyielding, as ingrained military training kicked in. The first order of business was cutting through Addison's panic. His vision narrowed to her slender form as everything else disappeared. "Addison, don't move."

She stilled immediately. Her head lifted and their gazes

met. The fear in her eyes cut him to the core, but he shoved the emotion to the side. Jason firmly planted his feet and extended his other hand. The windowsill dug deeper into his midsection, hard enough to leave a bruise. "Give me your other hand."

She reached up and Jason grasped hold of her wrist. Relief at having two points of contact registered somewhere in the depths of his brain, but the mission was only half over. "I'm going to pull you up. Plant your feet against the wall and walk upward toward me."

Jason hinged back. He'd kept up a workout routine after the bombing, but his body had never returned to its previous strength. The pin holding his leg together, along with the scarred and damaged arm muscles, screamed with agony. He gritted his teeth against the pain and continued to move.

Addison did as he instructed, using the wall to walk toward the window. His grip on her hand and wrist was vise-like. Dropping her was not an option.

Addison's upper body reached the window. Jason shifted his hold to her waist and yanked her the rest of the way into the apartment. They collapsed in a heap on the floor. He barely felt the glass from the broken window under his body. Or the carpeting. The only thing he could register was the sensation of Addison in his arms.

She was okay. She was alive.

Jason kissed her. Emotions erupted in a heady mix he'd never experienced before as Addison returned his passion. This woman unraveled him. She touched something inside him Jason thought had died years ago in the dry desert of a country half a world away. Try as he might, he couldn't resist her.

The wail of sirens filtered through the open window,

bringing him back to the reality of the moment. He broke off the kiss, breathless, and then rose. Jason brushed his lips against Addison's one more time before scooping her into his arms and carrying her over the glass so her bare feet wouldn't be cut.

An hour later, Jason and Addison were sitting on the bumper of his SUV waiting, once again, to speak to a detective. Firefighters and police officers moved around the parking lot. Crime scene tape fluttered in the breeze. Chloe's apartment was destroyed, and a search was underway to locate her.

Addison's emergency blanket crinkled as she laid her head on Jason's shoulder. Her feet swung back and forth. She was wearing Jason's spare tennis shoes, and they were several sizes too big. "Do you think the arsonist was after me? Or Chloe?"

"I'm not sure." He wrapped his arm around Addison, tucking her close to his side. "I've been wondering the same thing. Hopefully, finding Chloe will answer that."

"I'm worried about her."

"So am I." He brushed his mouth across her temple. "You saved my life today."

Her nose wrinkled. "That still leaves us three to one."

Jason chuckled, wrapping his other arm around her for a sideways hug. "We can call it even."

Someone called out his name. Jason turned his head. Texas Ranger Grady West strolled toward them on lanky strides. He wore a white button-down and khakis covered by a suit jacket. A cowboy hat shaded Grady's eyes from the sun.

Despite the seriousness of the situation, Jason grinned. He rose to greet the lawman. "Grady, I sure am glad to see you."

They shook hands and patted each other on the back in a manly embrace. Grady's eyes were shadowed with concern, but his mouth quirked up. "What is it with you and burning buildings, Jason? This is your second incident with one. You should've been a firefighter."

They shared a laugh. Jason had run into a burning cabin to help Grady rescue his then girlfriend, Tara. The event itself wasn't something to joke about, but Grady—like Jason and his friends—sometimes used dark humor to cope with the aftermath of dangerous situations. Thankfully, Grady's story had a happy ending. He and Tara were married with two beautiful children. One of them was Jason's goddaughter, Maddy.

Addison appeared at Jason's side. He wrapped an arm around her waist. "Grady, I'd like you to meet Addison. Addison, this is Grady West."

She extended her hand toward Grady, a bright smile on her lips. "It's so nice to meet you. Jason has told me wonderful things about your family. Maddy, especially. He has a soft spot for his goddaughter."

Grady shook her hand warmly. "It's a pleasure to meet you too, although I'm sorry it's not under better circumstances."

"So am I."

Grady turned his attention to Jason. "It's good you called. I requested and received permission from the Austin Police Department to lead the investigation into this attack. Chief Walters won't be happy, but he doesn't have a say anymore. Based on the evidence and the previous attacks on Addison, I have a responsibility to investigate everything."

A weight Jason didn't realize he was carrying lifted from his shoulders. "That's the best news I've heard in a long time. Given Chloe's disappearance and the way Michael

145

McCormick was acting at the courthouse today, I believe he's involved."

"I agree." Addison's gaze drifted to the smoldering apartment building behind Grady. "But proving it won't be easy. Michael was at court, surrounded by a judge and his attorneys when the fire started."

Jason's jaw tightened. "Have you spoken with the responding officers? Do you have any idea how the fire was set?"

Grady nodded. "The perpetrator was hiding in the empty apartment across from Chloe's. He waited for you and Addison to go inside, and then he spread gasoline and lit a match."

That answered one question. The attack was designed to kill Addison, not Chloe. It'd almost succeeded. Jason couldn't make heads or tails of it. Had they been wrong about Wendall's involvement?

"If I was the target, how does Wendall fit into all of this?" Addison asked, echoing Jason's thoughts. "And where is Chloe?"

"I've got officers and troopers scouring every part of the city, searching for Chloe and her vehicle." Grady's brow furrowed. "We need to be careful about jumping to conclusions. Although there have been previous threats on your life, this attack may not be connected to the others. Can you think of any reason why Wendall would benefit from hurting Chloe?"

Addison shook her head. "Not directly, but whoever is behind these attacks has been stalking me for a while. It wouldn't take much effort to know Chloe's divorce trial was happening this afternoon. Wendall could've kidnapped or hurt Chloe, hoping that I'd show up at the apartment. But that seems a lot of trouble to go to."

Jason nodded. "I agree. The person who benefits the most from hurting Chloe and Addison is Michael."

Grady opened his mouth as if to say something, but his phone rang. He removed it from his belt, excused himself, and stepped away to answer it.

Addison turned to Jason, rose on her tiptoes, and brushed a kiss across his mouth. "Thank you for calling Grady. He's as wonderful as you said, and I feel a lot better knowing he's on the case."

"So do I." Jason ran a thumb over the curve of Addison's cheek, relishing in being close to her. Holding her. "You're covered in soot."

She smiled, the corners of her gorgeous eyes crinkling. "I'm not the only one, Marine."

Grady ran up to them. "Officers located Chloe. She's being transported to the hospital."

TWENTY-FIVE

The hospital emergency room was pandemonium. A five car pileup on the freeway had resulted in numerous injuries. Addison hurried to keep pace with Grady's long strides, her progress hindered by the oversized tennis shoes on her feet. Jason's shoes. A reminder of how perilously close they'd come to losing their lives.

Her throat was sore from the smoke inhalation and every single one of her muscles ached. Especially her shoulders. But all of that paled in comparison to the worry eating away at her insides. Chloe had been attacked on her way to the courthouse, but the extent of her injuries wasn't clear.

Jason placed a hand on the small of Addison's back. His touch was warm. Comforting. Everything about the man was comforting. No one else could've calmed Addison down the way Jason had when she fell from the ledge. Their connection was beyond anything she'd ever experienced.

Grady flashed his badge at the front desk and asked for Chloe. Within short order, a nurse escorted them into the interior area of the hospital. "She's been asking for you specifically, Ms. Foster, and was quite insistent we call your office. No one could locate you. Then one of the patrol officers mentioned that Chloe's apartment caught fire with you inside and she was beside herself."

Addison's hand flew to her jacket pocket, but it was empty. "I don't have my cell with me."

She'd shoved her phone in the side pocket of her briefcase at the courthouse. The same one she'd handed to Rachel. Her paralegal was probably frantic with worry. Addison made a mental note to send Rachel a text from Jason's phone at the earliest opportunity.

Grady stopped outside the door leading to an exam room. "Addison, go in first and introduce me. Chloe will feel more comfortable with your presence."

His consideration touched Addison. Jason might be selective with his friends, but he knew how to pick the best ones. She'd just met the Texas Ranger, but so far, he'd been both capable and kind. It was a tremendous relief to have him leading the investigation into the attacks.

Addison slipped into the room, followed by Grady and Jason. Chloe glanced up as they entered and gasped. A hand flew to her mouth. "Addison, thank God you're okay."

She started to sit up and Addison hurried over to stop her. Chloe's face was bruised along one side as if she'd been struck several times. A scrape followed the graceful line of her neck and her left arm was encased in a cast.

Addison gently hugged her. "I'm fine, Chloe, but you look a bit worse for the wear. What happened?"

"Someone attacked me on my way to court." Chloe's bottom lip trembled. "Michael has to be behind this. He threatened to kill me if I ever left and now he's making good on that promise. I'm so sorry, Addison. I never should've dragged you into this. It's been a giant mess from the beginning."

"I told you before. You have nothing to apologize for. This isn't your fault." Addison gestured to the men standing quietly near the door. "But you can help us with the investigation. Grady is a Texas Ranger. He's a friend of Jason's and someone we can trust."

Grady stepped forward, removing his cowboy hat and tipping his head toward Chloe. "Texas Ranger Grady West. Ma'am, I'm very sorry about what's happened to you. I promise to do everything in my power to catch the man responsible."

Chloe tugged Addison down and whispered, "Are you sure we can trust him?"

"Yes. I know this is hard, but think of Stella. We need law enforcement's help to protect you and your baby."

Chloe hesitated and then nodded, but there was a lingering wariness in her eyes. She let out a long breath. "I don't know how much I can help you, Mr. West. Or is it Texas Ranger West?"

"Grady is just fine, ma'am." He settled the hat back on his head before removing a pad and pen from his suit jacket. "Let's start by walking through your morning."

"It was normal. I got my daughter, Stella, dressed for the day and took her to my mother's before returning to the apartment. I got ready for court and left. As I was driving, I heard a thumping coming from the car. I pulled into the nearest parking lot and discovered my tire was flat."

Addison passed a glance toward Jason and saw her own thoughts reflected in his expression. The attacker had waited until Chloe went back to the apartment and then sabotaged her car. There was no doubt this was a well-planned attack.

"I was about to call triple A," Chloe continued, "when

another vehicle raced into the parking lot. A man dressed in all black and a ski mask—"

Her voice broke off. She was clutching Addison's hand so tightly, the bones rubbed together. Addison was tempted to halt the interview since it appeared Chloe was on the verge of a panic attack. She'd been through a lot.

"Take your time," Grady said, his tone patient and sympathetic. "We can go as slowly as you need."

His words had the right effect. Chloe took several deep breaths and her hold on Addison's hand relaxed. She licked her lips. "The man in the ski mask punched me in the face, which was enough to disorient me. He dragged me into his vehicle. I waited for him to start driving, and then I jumped from the car." She lifted the cast. "That's how I broke my arm."

"Can you describe the attacker?"

"Not really. He was about your height. Strong." She bit her lip. "It all happened so fast. I don't remember much."

"What about the vehicle he was driving? Do you know what kind it was?"

"An SUV. I'm not very good with cars, so I can't tell you the make and model. It was dark blue, though, and older." Her eyes widened slightly. "And it had some kind of decal on the front windshield. It looked like a gremlin holding a cigarette."

Addison inhaled sharply, her muscles tightening involuntarily. Wendall's SUV. Her father-in-law had attacked Chloe. Could he be working with Michael? She didn't know of any connection between the two men, but it was the only thing that made sense.

Grady walked Chloe through the attack several times, but she couldn't provide additional information. She twisted the sheet with her hand. "I don't know what to do.

The hospital is going to release me. I can't go back to my apartment, and I'm too scared to stay at my mom's."

"I can provide protection for you, ma'am. We have safe houses—"

"No." Her tone was sharp. Chloe seemed to catch herself because she closed her eyes and waited a beat before reopening them. "I'm sorry, Grady. You seem like a nice man, but my husband has connections in law enforcement. I don't trust you completely."

"I may have a solution." Jason stepped forward. "My grandfather left me a cabin near Huntsville. It's difficult to find and off the beaten path. You and your family will be safe there. My friend, Kyle, can go with you to provide protection. He's former military. I would trust him with my life."

"So would I," Addison said.

Chloe scanned both their faces before slowly nodding. "I don't have many options, and I'll do anything to keep my daughter safe. I would like to meet Kyle beforehand though."

Jason took out his phone. "I'll text him to come to the hospital. There's no pressure, Chloe. If you don't want Kyle to go with you, the offer of the cabin still stands. We can arrange for private security, perhaps. But that might take time and I would prefer if you were with someone I trusted."

The tension in her shoulders dropped even more. "Thank you, Jason. I agree it would be better to be with someone you know. Please ask Kyle to come and meet me. I'll decide after he and I talk."

Jason made the arrangements and then he and Grady stepped out into the hall. Addison made sure Chloe was settled before joining them. From the way Chloe's eyes were drifting shut, she was going to sleep for a while.

The hallway smelled like a mixture of bleach and corn dogs. Phones rang in the nurse's station. Addison waited until the door to Chloe's room closed completely before turning toward the two men. "I think Wendall and Michael are working together. It's the only explanation that makes sense and fits with the evidence we have."

Grady's expression was pensive. "Is there any connection between the two men?"

"Not to my knowledge. But Michael is smart and ruthless. I guarantee, once I became Chloe's attorney, he researched me. Maybe even hired private investigators. He could've discovered Wendall that way."

"We considered Michael had hired a hit man," Jason added. "Wendall would be a good candidate. He already hates Addison. Throw in a pile of cash and it's a no-brainer for a criminal like him."

Grady nodded. "I agree it makes sense, but right now, it's all conjecture. We don't have evidence Wendall and Michael are working together."

Addison's insides turned cold. "Finding it won't be easy. And since kidnapping Chloe failed, both Michael and Wendall will be desperate. They'll attack again. Soon."

TWENTY-SIX

There was nothing worse than waiting for the enemy to make a move.

Jason parted the curtains on a window in Addison's living room and stared into the yard. A shadow moved along the tree line.

Nathan. The Green Beret had taken the first shift patrolling the area around Addison's house. Grady had also stationed a state trooper to sit on the street. Combined with the state-of-the-art security system, Addison's home was secure. And yet, unease knitted Jason's muscles. He agreed with Addison's assessment at the hospital. Michael and Wendall were growing increasingly desperate. They would try something again, and soon.

The question was: what?

Connor nudged his arm. The scar along the side of his body was darker than the surrounding hair. Jason stroked his dog's head. "You feel it too, huh, buddy?"

The patter of footsteps on the hardwood preceded Addison into the room. She'd showered, exchanging her smoke-filled clothes for a comfy set of yoga pants and a long T-shirt. Thick socks covered her feet. She wasn't wearing makeup and her hair was left loose. It flowed like a silk curtain of curls around her shoulders and down her back. Jason's heart clenched at the sight of her.

Connor jogged over to greet Addison. She planted a kiss in between the dog's eyes, talking to him in a low and soothing voice. Jason couldn't make out the words, but Connor's tail swiped across the floor in a steady rhythm. The dog loved Addison.

He wasn't the only one. Addison had wriggled her way into Jason's heart and there was no turning back. She was gorgeous—there was no question about that—but it went far deeper than her looks. Her innate kindness, her bravery, her faith...everything about her pulled Jason closer.

He would do anything for her. Anything.

Addison smiled and gestured to the coffee table. Hot tea sat steaming in mugs next to slices of apple pie straight from Nelson's Diner. "Is that for us? Where did you get the pie?"

"I called the owner and asked him for a favor. He had one of his busboys deliver the pie. After today, I figured you deserved some TLC." He took one last glance out of the window before releasing the curtain. Everything was quiet.

Addison snagged a plate. She used her fork to cut through the flaky crust and tender apples before taking a bite. She made a throaty hum of satisfaction. "This is even better than the one Kyle brought. Thank you, Jason."

"Wait until you try their chocolate silk pie." He grinned. "It'll make you weep with happiness."

She scowled playfully. "You told me apple was the best."

"It is, but you can never go wrong with any of the

desserts." Jason picked up his own plate. "Did you reach Chloe? How is she?"

"Better." Addison sank onto the couch, absently reaching out to stroke Shelby. The cat was curled up on the arm of the sofa. "Kyle and Chloe have hit it off. She sounded a lot less stressed than when we spoke to her at the hospital. They've reached the cabin and are settling in."

"I think it's a good thing only a few of us know where she is. I'm sure that makes Chloe feel safer."

"It does. Has there been any news from Grady?"

"He's got every officer in the state looking for Wendall. Undercover police are watching Michael, so if he makes a move, we'll know about it. Grady went and spoke to Steven as well, but didn't get any additional information out of him."

Addison's hand slowed as it traveled down the cat's back. "Steven. I don't know what to think about him. Part of me is sympathetic, but another part is angry."

"That's reasonable. He betrayed your trust. You were in danger, Steven knew about it and said nothing. I think that would make anyone angry."

"I suppose you're right."

Jason joined her on the couch. Connor settled at their feet with a sigh. The lamp light cast a warm glow over Addison's features. She picked at the pie with her fork. "The cabin Chloe's staying at...is that the one you go to every year?"

"It is. My grandfather built it. He used to take me there as a kid and we'd spend our days hiking and fishing. That's why I go there on the anniversary of the bombing. The cabin reminds me of when life was simple. Before things got so hard."

Addison set her pie on the table and turned to face him. "We never finished the conversation on my porch. I know this isn't the best timing in the world, but after nearly dying today, I don't want one more minute to go by without saying this. I'm falling in love with you, Jason."

He inhaled sharply. Hope bloomed followed by a bone-crushing fear. "Addy..."

"Wait, let me finish. I understand you're trying to protect me, but I don't need you to. I'm a grown woman, capable of making my own decisions. I get that the PTSD is a part of you. But so is your courage, your thoughtfulness. Your ability to create beautiful paintings. I'm not interested in only taking the good without the bad."

No, she wouldn't be. It's what made this so difficult.

Jason tucked a strand of silky hair behind her ear. "It's not that simple, Addy. There are no guarantees, and while there are steps I can take to control my PTSD, nothing is foolproof. I don't want to mislead you."

"You haven't. If anything you've been brutally honest. What happened this afternoon was a crash course in how extreme your PTSD can get." She cupped his cheek. "I'm not scared."

"Why not?"

"Because together, with our faith, we can do anything. Today was an example of that in action. You needed me; I needed you." She smiled, softly. "And we both needed God."

He ran a thumb over the curve of her cheek. Addison made a compelling argument and Jason wanted to dive headfirst into these feelings, but the vivid memory of his flashback prevented him. "Let's make a deal. No promises. Not until the threat is over. Then we can talk again."

"You're worried I'll change my mind."

"I wouldn't blame you one bit if you did." He brushed a kiss across her mouth. She tasted like apple pie. Light, sweet, and undemanding. "And I have my own baggage to clean up. You may not care about my PTSD, but I do. I need to get myself right with God about it."

"Okay." This time, it was her turn to lean in and kiss him. "But just so you know, I'm not changing my mind."

"No promises, Addy." He reluctantly let her go and handed her a mug of tea. "Here. It's getting cold."

They spent the next half hour eating pie, drinking tea, and talking. Jason kept the rest of the conversation light, telling Addison funny stories about when Connor was a puppy. At some point, Shelby moved from the arm of the sofa to their legs. The cat splayed her body across them both. Her rumbling purrs were soothing.

It was cozy. Homey. It was easy to imagine a life with Addison just like this one. Laughing and eating pie with Connor at their feet and Shelby in their laps. A wedding. A baby. Grandchildren. It was a life Jason had deemed impossible after returning from Afghanistan.

Had he been wrong?

A wash of unexpected guilt swept over him. Jason was thinking about falling in love and moving on with his life, while his comrades never made it home. They would never kiss their loved one or see their kids grow.

It didn't sit right. In fact, it felt downright awful. Jason pulled away from Addison under the guise of setting his plate on the coffee table. Anxiety swirled in his stomach and the taste of the pie turned sour.

A knock came on the front door. Jason's head swiveled in that direction. "Were you expecting someone?"

Addison frowned, worry flickering in her eyes. "No."

"Stay here." Jason rose from the couch. His hand drifted to his weapon as he approached the door at an angle. "Who is it?"

"It's Trevor, Jason. Open up. I need to speak to you and Addison."

TWENTY-SEVEN

"You were right." Trevor removed his hat as he entered Addison's house. His police uniform was sharply pressed, but circles shadowed the area under his eyes. "The fire chief determined the explosion at the abandoned store was a bomb."

Jason shut the door behind Trevor. He wasn't surprised by the conclusion, but he was grateful for it all the same. It solidified everything they'd been saying.

Addison rose from the couch, concern creasing the space between her brows. Trevor greeted her with a hug. "I'm sorry to drop by so late and unannounced, but I thought you should know what the fire chief said." He released her and backed up a few steps. "I owe both of you an apology."

Addison crossed her arms over her chest. "And what about Michael McCormick?"

"Given the attack on you and Chloe today, he's become a person of interest in this case." Trevor glanced at Jason. "I met with Texas Ranger Grady West. His reputation in law enforcement is impeccable. Chief Walters wasn't happy to have him interfering in the case, but I'm grateful for his help."

Some of the tension in Jason's shoulders loosened. Chief Walters had a personal relationship with Michael and it was clouding his judgment. It would've been difficult for Trevor to go against his boss, especially without hard evidence. Jason understood the chain of command and the embedded loyalties that went with it better than most. He held no ill will against the detective.

"What can you tell us about the bomb?" Addison asked.

"It had a remote detonator, so it could be set off using a cell phone. We've sent the evidence to the state lab for analysis. So far, we haven't recovered any fingerprints, but they aren't done yet."

Jason frowned. Building a bomb with a remote detonator wasn't complicated, but it took some technological knowledge. "Chloe mentioned to us that Michael was a bomb enthusiast. How sophisticated was the device?"

Trevor shrugged. "I'm not sure yet. We've pulled surveillance video from the surrounding businesses, but none of them have an unrestricted view of the abandoned store. However, a witness described a late-model SUV with a decal on the windshield in the area a few hours before the Winter Fair."

"Wendall's vehicle." Addison started pacing. "How is it possible his SUV keeps showing up, but no one has seen Wendall in weeks? It doesn't make any sense. It feels like we're chasing a ghost."

It did feel that way. Something niggled the back of Jason's mind, but he couldn't grab hold of the idea.

Trevor tracked Addison with his gaze. "I would feel better if you were in a secure location. My parents own a vacation home in Colorado. You're more than welcome to it."

Addison paused midstep. "Thank you, Trevor, but I feel more comfortable here. I have Jason and Nathan watching out for me, along with a state trooper. Plus the security system on the house is state-of-the-art."

He hesitated and then nodded. "Okay. If you change your mind, let me know. I'll call if there are any more updates."

After Trevor left, Addison rubbed her forehead, as if a headache was creeping up on her. Circles shadowed the delicate skin under her eyes. She looked exhausted and vulnerable.

"Why don't you take an aspirin and go to bed, Addy?" Jason tucked his hands in his pockets to avoid pulling her into his arms. "I'll clean the dishes."

She lowered her hand and gave him a weak smile. "Thanks. I've been fighting a headache all day."

From the stress no doubt. Addison stepped closer and brushed her lips across his cheek. Then she collected Shelby from the couch and headed into the bedroom. Jason watched her go, a mixture of feelings tumbling around inside him. Connor nudged his hand.

"Right, buddy. Dishes."

Jason cleared the coffee table, carrying the dirty dishes into the kitchen. He loaded the dishwasher. Wiped the counter. Prepared the coffee pot for later. The chores did little to stop the thoughts and questions rolling through his mind. Sleep would be impossible.

He shrugged on a jacket, unarmed the security system, and slipped onto the porch with Connor. The night air was crisp and scented with dried leaves and grass. Jason used his phone to rearm the alarm. The glow from the motion detection lights faded as he crossed the yard. His eyes adjusted to the dark. An owl swept down from a tree, the flap of wings cutting through the quiet.

Nathan greeted him with a chin jerk. "No sign of trouble."

"Good."

Jason tucked his hands into the pockets of his jacket. He and Nathan stood side by side, silent, for a good long while. The sky was cloud free. The moon was a smooth crescent, surrounded by a scattering of stars. Jason took a deep breath and let it out slowly. "Do you think God has a plan for all of us?"

"You're feeling philosophical tonight."

"Addison said she's falling in love with me. It has me questioning things."

Nathan grunted. "Because you've been spending the last three years punishing yourself for surviving a bombing when the others didn't."

"Yeah, something like that." The cold air stung Jason's lungs and made his chest tighten. "I failed them, Nathan. Logically, I know it's not my fault. But...moving on, being happy, feels like a betrayal."

"Being miserable won't bring them back." Nathan was quiet for a long moment. "I'm gonna tell you something that may be hard for you to hear, but it's the truth. We're soldiers. We all knew the score when we went overseas. If your fellow Marines were here now, they'd tell you the same. Grieve their deaths but don't dishonor their memory by using it as a crutch to keep from living your life."

Jason reared back. "Is that what you think I'm doing?"

"You made it home. They didn't. You owe it to them to live the best life possible."

Nathan's words struck a hard blow, and Jason's throat

clogged with emotion as heat pricked the back of his eyes. He'd been carrying an albatross of guilt and responsibility. It never occurred to him it was the wrong burden.

"To answer your question, yes, I believe God has a plan for all of us," Nathan continued. "Addison is an amazing person. It's clear the two of you care for each other deeply. That kind of relationship doesn't come around every day. Trust me, if you let her go, you'll regret it for the rest of your life."

Jason rocked back on his heels. He knew some of Nathan's story. He'd broken up with his fiancée after joining the Green Berets. It wasn't something Nathan talked about often, and Jason hadn't realized his friend regretted breaking things off. "It sounds like you're speaking from experience."

"I am. But we aren't talking about me. We're talking about you." Nathan breathed out and a fog hung in front of his face. "Be careful with the choice you make, Jason. Once you break her heart, you won't be able to repair the damage later."

Nathan's warning echoed Jason's own instincts. He was falling in love with Addison and the very last thing he wanted to do was screw it up. He needed to think and pray. "Do you want to head inside for some shut-eye, Nathan? I can take over for a while."

"Naw, you go in." Nathan clapped him on the shoulder. "I've got this."

Jason nodded, exhaustion seeping into his bones. He started across the yard and then turned back. "Hey, Nathan, have you tried asking for forgiveness? It might not repair the damage, but it's a good place to start."

His friend was quiet for a long moment. "Some things aren't easily forgivable. But I'll keep your advice in mind."

Whatever was bothering Nathan, Jason could tell his friend didn't want to discuss it. Never mind. Nathan would talk when he was ready.

Jason patted his leg and Connor joined him. They went back inside Addison's house. Her couch was too short for his tall frame, so he settled for the recliner. Jason kept his boots on, his gun close, and his cell phone in his hand. If there was trouble, Nathan would call.

He rubbed his chest, trying to dislodge the pain in his heart. But it wouldn't budge.

God, I'm ready to listen. I've been fighting You, throwing out excuses to keep from falling in love with Addison, and doing my best to keep her at arm's length. But You knew better.

It was time. Time to let go of the pain and do what God intended—live his life. His fellow Marines would always be a part of him. Like the scars etched on his skin, their memories were carved in his heart. But Jason would not disgrace their sacrifice by rejecting Addison and her love out of some twisted sense of obligation.

Somehow, sleep claimed him. The sound of his ringtone brought him awake instantly. It was pitch-black outside the windows and a quick glance at the clock confirmed it was a little after one in the morning. Jason answered the call.

"We've got company."

Nathan's words were followed by an eruption of gunshots.

TWENTY-EIGHT

Addison's eyes flew open and she gasped. Jason hovered over her, his finger at his lips, indicating she should be quiet.

"There's trouble," he whispered. "Put your shoes on."

Addison sat up in bed, shoving her covers aside. She'd slept in her clothes. The lamp on the nightstand cast the room in a soft glow as she slid her feet into tennis shoes. Her heart thundered against her rib cage and her fingers trembled as she did the laces. Connor, sensing her tension, licked her cheek. She rubbed a hand over his soft fur.

Jason went to her bedroom window. His gun was in one hand and he used the other to part the curtains. Addison joined him. "What happened?"

"I don't know." He kept his gaze locked on the yard beyond the glass. "Nathan said there was a problem. Then there were gunshots."

More tension poured into her muscles. "You have to help him."

"No, Nathan is an experienced soldier. My job is to protect you." His tone brooked no argument. "I've called 911. Officers are on the way."

That wasn't good enough. Soldier or not, Nathan was in danger because of her. Addison would never forgive herself if he was hurt or killed while they stood by. Not to mention the trooper stationed outside her house. "It'll take time for responding officers to get here, and by then it may be too late."

Jason's phone beeped with an incoming text. He glanced at the screen and tried to hide it from Addison's view, but she caught sight of the message. It was from Nathan.

SOS.

The universal request for help. Addison shook Jason's arm, urgency fueling the movement. "Go. The house is secure. It has an alarm and the attacker knows it, otherwise he would've broken in. I'm safe here."

Jason stubbornly didn't respond, but a muscle in his jaw worked. This was as difficult for him as it was for her. Maybe worse. He blamed himself for what happened in Afghanistan. Standing around while Nathan was in trouble went against everything Jason had trained for. Addison couldn't bear the thought of adding to his pain.

She met his gaze. "The choice is mine, Jason. It's my life and I want you to go."

He kissed her, quick but gentle. "Hide in the bathroom and lock the door. Give me thirty seconds to get out of the house and then use your cell to rearm the alarm behind me. I'm leaving Connor with you too."

Addison grabbed her cell phone and mace. Connor followed her into the bathroom and Jason gave him the order to guard. Then he grabbed Addison's hand. "Don't open this door for anyone other than me. You got it?"

She nodded. Her gaze swept over him. Jason's dark hair was mussed, the faint night-light caressing the scars on his cheek. Her warrior. There was so much Addison wanted to say, but there wasn't time. She brushed her thumb over the back of his hand. "Be careful."

In a heartbeat, he was gone. Addison flipped the lock. Her gaze fell on the chair in front of the vanity. For extra measure, she shoved that under the doorknob.

Convinced she was as secure as possible, Addison sank to the bathmat on the floor. She counted thirty seconds out in her head and then used her cell to re-engage the house alarm. Connor joined her on the mat.

"We're gonna be okay, boy." She stroked his back, using the repetitious pattern to slow her breathing. Addison used her cell phone to scroll through the footage of the cameras on her house. The trooper's vehicle wasn't on the street. Other than that, everything looked normal, although she knew it wasn't. Prayers fell from her lips in whispered words. They were all she could provide to help Jason, Nathan, and the trooper.

Connor growled.

Addison froze. She held her breath, straining to listen beyond the closed door.

Silence.

Connor rose from beside her on the mat and took a protective stance in front of her. The hair on the back of his neck rose. She didn't know how it was possible, but someone was inside the house. Connor wouldn't behave that way if it was Jason or Nathan.

Addison used her phone to activate the alert panic button on her home alarm system. Jason had already called the police, and they were supposedly on the way, but so far, she hadn't heard any sirens. Her mind raced, struggling to make sense of the impossible. Then it hit her. They'd disarmed the alarm when Jason left the house. It was only a moment, but it would've been long enough for someone to slip inside using another door without being noticed.

Addison stood and gripped her mace. The only illumination in the bathroom came from the night-light. Maybe the intruder would be fooled into thinking she'd left with Jason...

Another growl rumbled low in Connor's chest as a creak came from the bedroom. Addison's pulse jumped. Her gaze shot to the doorknob.

It began to turn.

———

Jason sprinted through the woods behind Addison's house. The flash of blue-and-red lights from the trooper's patrol car acted as a beacon directing his path. The vehicle was parked on the dirt road. The attacker had used the escape route several times. Chances were the trooper and Nathan had discovered him, hence the exchange of gunfire.

Jason kept his gaze sharp as he ran toward the patrol car. Branches tugged at his clothes. His boots pounded against the ground, the sound muffled by leaves and pine needles. Nathan had to be injured. And badly. He wouldn't have sent an SOS message otherwise. Leaving Addison in the house had been a calculated risk. She was secure behind the alarm system and she had Connor as backup. The German shepherd would protect her with his life if necessary.

No. It wouldn't come to that. Addison was safe. Jason did his best to shove the doubts from his mind and focus on the task at hand—saving his brother. Nathan wasn't his flesh and blood, but might as well be. Jason couldn't bear the thought of losing him.

Please, God. I've made so many mistakes. Guide me to make the right ones now.

He halted at the edge of the road. Jason tightened the hold on his weapon as he assessed the situation. The trooper's vehicle was sitting at an angle, driver's side door open. The squawk of the radio broke through the stillness of the night.

Someone moaned.

The sound came from the other side of the car. Jason would have to step into the road to gain a vantage point. It put him at risk if a sniper was hiding in the trees, but there wasn't a choice.

Bracing himself for the sound of gunfire, Jason slipped out of the woods. He raised his gun and circled the trooper's vehicle.

"Don't try it." The command, little more than a growl, came from behind the trooper's open door. The barrel of a gun was visible. It was pointed straight at Jason's chest.

"Nathan, it's me."

"Jason." The gun disappeared. "We need paramedics."

Jason continued around the door and his friend came into view. Blood coated the side of Nathan's face, more covered his pants. Beside him was the trooper. The man was unconscious and badly injured. Nathan had removed his shirt and was using it as a pressure bandage against the trooper's chest.

"Paramedics are on the way." Jason crouched next to the law enforcement officer and felt for a pulse. A heartbeat thumped against his fingers. Relief flooded over him. "What happened?"

"Ambush." Nathan grimaced. "The trooper was attacked first. I intervened, and the shooter hit me too."

Jason's gaze swept across his friend. Nathan had been

shot in the leg. Judging from the amount of blood, the bullet had nicked an artery. Jason quickly removed his belt and then wrapped the leather around his friend's leg as a makeshift tourniquet. "Did you see who it was?"

Nathan leaned his head against the car. "No, but he was aiming to kill. One bullet must've grazed my head. It knocked me out. I think the shooter thought I was dead. I came to moments before you arrived."

Jason's head jerked up. "What? No, Nathan. You must've been conscious longer than you thought. You sent me a text message."

"No, I didn't." His hand flew to his pocket. "My cell is gone."

Sheer panic shot through Jason's veins. If Nathan didn't have his cell phone, then the shooter did.

It'd been a trap.

Jason shot to his feet. "Addison."

He bolted for the trees. Addison's house was barely visible through the thick branches. Jason plowed through them, desperation fueling his steps.

No. No. No.

Jason burst free of the tree line and raced across the yard. He didn't bother with disarming the security system or unlocking the door. He shoved his boot against the lock, breaking the door down in one kick.

A gunshot echoed through the house followed by a scream.

Addison.

Jason bolted for the back bedroom. The sound of crashing glass came down the hall as he surged across the threshold. The window in Addison's room was broken, a dark shadow escaping across the yard. There was no time to give chase. All he cared about was Addison.

Heart thundering, he slid to a stop in the bathroom doorway. The door was hanging from the hinges, boot marks embedded in the wood from being broken down. A chair had been thrown across the room. It rested legs up on the tile. Addison held a towel in one hand, mace poised to spray in the other. Her shirt was spattered with blood. She registered Jason's presence and tears streamed down her face.

"You're hurt." He reached for her. Adrenaline could mask pain. "You've been shot."

"No, it's not me."

She shifted. Jason's chest tightened so much it was impossible to draw in a breath and time slowed as his vision narrowed. Pain, as vibrant as the day of the bombing in Afghanistan, vibrated through him.

Connor lay on the bathmat, blood coating his fur.

TWENTY-NINE

Addison pressed her foot against the accelerator, pushing her Honda Civic as much as she dared on the dark country road. The closest emergency vet was twenty minutes away from her house. She cast a quick glance in the rearview mirror. Jason was stroking Connor's muzzle with one hand, while applying pressure to stop the wound from bleeding with the other.

Tears pricked the back of Addison's eyelids, but she clamped down on her emotions. She couldn't fall apart. Not now. Later, there would be time to cry.

She fixed her gaze back on the road, pushing even more on the accelerator. Addison flipped on her brights to ward off animals. "How's he doing?"

"Breathing is steady. Heart rate too. The gunshot looks like a through and through." Jason's voice was calm, but worry rode the warm timbres of his tone. "It's still bleeding, but it's manageable. How far till we get to the vet?"

"Ten minutes. Hang in there, Connor." She gripped the steering wheel. "He saved my life. Without even thinking about it, he attacked."

LYNN SHANNON

"He's a soldier. It's his job to protect the innocent. He does it well."

She barely tapped the brakes as they rounded a curve. "It all happened so fast. I didn't even get a good look at the intruder. He was wearing all black and a ski mask."

"Nathan said the same."

Jason's phone beeped. Addison sensed rather than saw him check the message. She didn't take her gaze from the road. "What is it?"

"It's Kyle. Everything is quiet at the cabin."

"Michael and Wendall don't know where Chloe is, thank God."

Jason's phone rang. He answered and must've put the call on speaker, because Grady's voice was loud enough for Addison to hear. "Where are you, Jason?"

"Route 14, ten minutes from the vet's office."

The twinkling lights of the town were up ahead. Addison breathed a sigh of relief, but didn't lessen her pressure on the accelerator. She had to get Connor there as fast as possible.

"A trooper will be waiting for you at the emergency vet's office." Grady's tone was clipped. "You are to stay there until I tell you to move. Michael hasn't left his house, but I'm not taking any chances. We're still searching for Wendall."

Grady's next words were lost as an engine roared. Something slammed into the back of Addison's vehicle. The wheel jerked under her hands and she fought to wrestle it back under control before they skidded into the embankment. Bright lights flicked on, bouncing off the rearview mirror, blinding her.

Wendall. He'd found them.

174

Somewhere in the back of her mind, Addison heard Jason barking out information to Grady, but the words were a jumble. Her focus was on the road in front of them. A set of rapid curves approached with frightening speed. This section of the road was notoriously dangerous.

Wendall's vehicle kissed her bumper again. Addison swerved into the opposite lane, weaving to make them a harder target to hit. Her knuckles were white on the steering wheel. "Jason, hold tight to Connor."

She slammed on her brakes without warning. Wendall's SUV shot past them.

A horn exploded in the night. An oncoming car rounded a curve, heading straight for them. Addison jerked her wheel to avoid the collision but overcompensated. Her tires skidded off the edge of the road as the vehicle went into a spin. A whirl of trees rushed her.

Metal crunched followed by the sound of shattering glass. Addison's airbag exploded, smashing her in the face. Her seat belt pulled tight as the vehicle came to a shuttering stop. Pain erupted along her collarbone.

Silence.

It was extraordinarily loud in the wake of the crash. Addison shoved aside the airbag and sucked in a breath. Her hands shook violently. Tree branches pressed against the shattered windshield, the scent of pine filling her nostrils. One of her headlights was still working.

"Jason, are you and Connor okay?"

No response. Addison twisted in her seat. Her heart cried out, even as her mouth couldn't find the words. A large pine bough had shattered through the rear window and lodged itself in the car. Pine needles and smaller branches blocked her view of the back seat. Thousands of scenarios assaulted her, none of them good. The pine bough was so large, it could have seriously injured Jason, if not killed him.

Frantically, she shoved aside some of the branches, but it was impossible to see past them. "Jason, answer me!"

Silence. Tears coursed down her cheeks and her stomach swirled with nausea. Darkness beckoned at the edges of her vision. Addison fought it back, taking several deep breaths. She would not give up. She couldn't. If Jason was injured in the back of her vehicle, he needed her. She had to help him.

Please, Lord. Give me strength.

With shaking fingers, Addison hurried to unlock her seat belt. Every movement sent a wave of pain crashing over her. She took half a heartbeat to assess her physical condition. Her collarbone ached and there was a large lump on her head, hidden in her hair. She must've hit her head during the crash. That would explain the dizziness and nausea.

"Hang in there, Jason." She talked to him, hoping that he could hear her and was comforted, even if he couldn't respond. She fumbled for the door handle. Fresh tears welled in her eyes. "I'm in love with you. I know things have moved fast between us in the last few days, and no one is caught more off guard than I am, but I can't deny how I feel. I'm utterly, completely in love with you. And Connor too. Both of you, please, hang on."

A whimper came from the back seat.

Connor!

Addison's heart leapt as she struggled with the door handle. Nothing happened. She shoved against the unyielding door before realizing that a tree was blocking her exit. "Connor, I'm coming, sweetie. You brave, smart dog."

She ignored the pounding in her head and slid across the space between the driver's seat and the passenger's. Dizziness swamped her. Addison paused long enough to steady her vision and then grasped the handle. This time, the door flung open.

She stepped onto the ground and her knees gave way. Addison clung to the side of the vehicle. Her breath came in shallow bursts. Agony radiated across her chest. The pain was familiar. She'd experienced it after her husband tossed her down the stairs. She'd broken a rib. Maybe two.

It didn't matter. Connor and Jason needed her. Addison used the side of the Honda for support as she stumbled to the back door. Saying one last prayer, she opened it.

Jason was slouched, unconscious in the seat. Scratches marred his face and hands, one on his neck deep enough that blood stained the collar of his shirt and jacket. Connor was in his arms. Unlike his master, the German shepherd was alert. The large pine branch extended across them both, wedging them in place.

Connor whimpered. Addison caressed his head. "Hey, buddy. We're going to get you out of here."

She kept talking to Connor, even as her trembling hand went to Jason's wrist. The steady, strong beat of his heart tapped against her fingers. More tears flooded her vision as relief made her knees weak. "Thank you, Jesus. Thank you."

Jason groaned. Then his eyes slid open.

Addison's heart leapt for joy. She squeezed his wrist. "We've been in a car accident. You're stuck so don't try to move."

Something hard pressed against the back of Addison's head. The barrel of a gun. She froze, sensing someone behind her. Connor whimpered again. She suddenly understood that the dog had been trying to warn her.

Jason's gaze shifted from her face. Recognition flashed across his features and his lip curled in disgust. "Trevor."

THIRTY

Addison's heart thundered against her injured rib cage. "Trevor, I don't understand. What are you doing?"

He pressed the gun harder against her head. "Taking care of business. Where is Chloe?"

"You're working with Michael..." The implications ricocheted through her. All this time, Trevor was involved. Her mind raced to fit this new piece of information into what she already knew. "How could you?"

"I'm the one asking the questions, not you. Where is Chloe?"

Fear stalled her breath. Addison met Jason's gaze, finding strength and understanding in its depths. There was no way she would give Chloe's location. Not even with a gun pointed to her head.

Not even if it meant her death.

Could she stall? Jason had been talking to Grady on the phone when they had the accident. Surely the Texas Ranger was sending help. How long would it take them to arrive? A state trooper had been en route to the vet's office. If Grady called that trooper and diverted him here... She did a quick calculation in her muddled head. Help could arrive within minutes.

Minutes. She could do this. Addison licked her lips. "You were the one who broke into my house, weren't you?"

He was silent for a long moment. Then Trevor chuckled, low and mean. "Which time?"

"Both times. The bomb, the shooting, the attack at Chloe's apartment. Wendall was never involved, was he? You used my history with the Atkin family to fool us into believing Wendall was behind the threats."

"I always knew you were a smart one, Addy. It's a shame you didn't figure things out sooner."

She hadn't. Although she'd had an instinct about Trevor's involvement early on. The night they spoke on her porch, something had triggered her memories. But Addison had convinced herself that Trevor couldn't be involved. He was her friend and a police officer. He'd fooled her.

One question she'd never been able to answer was why the attacker used a black truck to run her down in the gym parking lot. Now she knew. Trevor had been on duty that day and his house was on the far side of town. He didn't have time to get the SUV, run her over in the parking lot, and return to his house. It'd also been daylight. Trevor couldn't risk someone seeing him driving the vehicle.

Betrayal burned her stomach, flooding her mouth with a sour taste. "How did you get your hands on Wendall's SUV?"

"He sold it to me. I gave him enough money to live like a king in Mexico."

Inside the vehicle, Jason shifted. He was wedged in place by the pine bough. Pain rippled across his features, and Addison felt like screaming. Jason and Connor needed medical attention. Where were the state police?

Please, Lord, I could use some help here.

"And Steven? What—"

"Enough chitchat. We're running out of time." He pressed the gun barrel against her head. "Where is Chloe?"

"I'm not telling you where she is, Trevor."

"Do you think I'm a fool?" Trevor grabbed her arm hard enough to leave bruises and whirled Addison around to face him. His expression was twisted and ugly. Pure evil. "This can go one of two ways. Hard will be painful. But if you cooperate, I'll make your death quick."

Her head spun as darkness crept in around the edges of her vision. Addison stumbled. The edge of the door, along with Trevor's hold on her arm, stopped her from falling. He shook her like a rag doll, with enough force to rattle her teeth.

A roar came from the Civic. Jason had lowered Connor and was shoving against the thick pine branch, but it wouldn't budge. His face was red with the effort. "Keep your hands off her."

Trevor laughed. "Looks like you're in no position to help. In fact—" He raised the gun and pointed it at Jason. His eyes were dark pits in the dim lighting, his mouth twisted with malevolence.

"No!" Addison shoved Trevor. The gun fired, but the shot went wide as he stumbled back.

He came around swinging with a curse. Trevor slammed the gun into the side of her face. Pain exploded across her cheek. Addison cried out. She fell to her knees against the hard-packed earth. Her stomach heaved and small rocks bit into the tender skin of her palms.

She sucked in a breath. Then another. The left side of her rib cage was on fire. She pressed a hand to her torso and a familiar bulge pressed against her palm.

Her mace! She'd put it in the pocket of her jacket.

"Trevor, I swear on my father's grave, I'll make you pay for this." Jason continued to shove against the tree branch, but it held him trapped.

Pain provided Addison with clarity. The large bough was wedged against the front passenger seat. If she shifted the chair forward, Jason might have enough room to get free.

Trevor ignored Jason's threats. He crouched next to Addison. He was wearing the same dark clothes as the intruder in her home, but this time, hadn't bothered with the ski mask. There was no need to. The road was empty. No one had driven past since their accident.

Her gaze lifted to the road. Wendall's SUV rested on the edge. She shivered.

"Yes, Addy, that's right. I've got it all planned out."

He would kill them. Then he would drive to the cabin and kill Chloe. Addison took a shallow breath. "You won't get away with it. Even if you frame Wendall, Grady believes Michael's involved."

"What he believes and what he can prove are two different matters. This will go better if you cooperate." Trevor placed the barrel of the gun under her chin and used it to force her head toward him. "Where is she, Addy?"

She glared at him, fingers fumbling for the edge of her pocket. "What did Michael promise you, Trevor? The chief of police position? It'll never work. When Grady solves this case, Michael will turn on you like a rat escaping a sinking ship."

He smirked. "Okay, have it your way."

He rose and walked over to the Honda. He raised his gun and pointed it at Jason.

Addison's heart stopped. She struggled to her feet. "Don't."

"Then tell me where she is, or I'll shoot him. First in the arm, then the leg. Ever been shot, Addy? It's excruciating."

"I'll tell you." Addison let the panic thrumming through her bleed into her voice. She met Jason's gaze briefly and then glanced at the front passenger seat. She hoped it was enough of a message that he would understand. "Chloe's in a cabin. Near Huntsville. There's no address. Give me your phone and I'll type in the coordinates."

Addison wrapped her fingers around the mace. Her insides quivered, but she forced herself to meet Trevor's gaze. He had to believe her lies. In order for the mace to work, she needed to be closer. She held her breath.

Please believe me. Please believe me.

Their lives depended on it.

Trevor dipped his hand into his pocket and then extended his phone toward her. "I want the exact location."

"Absolutely." Addison limped across the distance between them. Each breath enraged her broken ribs and sent fire through her body. She was in no position to fight Trevor in hand-to-hand combat, no matter how well she'd trained in boxing class. The mace was the only chance she had. Her hand tightened around the container.

Three.

Two.

One.

She held her breath and, with a swift movement, raised the mace while compressing the button. Trevor screamed as the chemicals hit his eyes. He stumbled back.

Addison spun on her heel. Every step was sheer torture, but she reached the Honda. Her fingers fumbled with the seat adjustment button. Sirens wailed in the distance. "Jason, I'm trying—"

Her finger found the right button and the seat flew forward on its track.

Footsteps pounded behind her. Addison turned, her pulse racing. Trevor was charging toward her like a murderous bull. His skin was mottled and red. Rage fueled his steps.

He was going to kill her.

A guttural roar came from the Honda as Jason leapt from the vehicle. He tackled Trevor, and both men tumbled to the ground. They wrestled for control of Trevor's gun. Addison's gaze swept the surrounding area, desperate to find some way to help Jason, but there was nothing.

The gun went off.

THIRTY-ONE

Three weeks later

Sunlight filtered through the trees, dappling the ground with intricate patterns. February was releasing her hold, giving way to springtime. A squirrel danced across the field in front of Jason's cabin and flowers poked free of the grass.

Jason drew in a deep breath. It smelled just as he remembered, like fresh pine and dirt. "It's not much to look at, but I promise it's better inside."

Addison passed him a skeptical glance. She'd tucked her hair into a ponytail and was dressed for their excursion to the cabin in jeans and hiking boots. The bruises from the car accident had finally faded, leaving her skin creamy and vibrant. "Chloe mentioned it was rustic. She didn't say how rustic."

He laughed, slipping his hand into hers. Beside him, Connor whined and shifted. His brown eyes were locked on the squirrel rooting through the grass.

Worry flared in Addison's expression. "Is Connor in pain?"

"No. He wants to chase the squirrel." Jason rubbed the dog's head. "Not yet, buddy. The vet said it'll be another couple of weeks before you're cleared to run."

It was a miracle Connor survived at all. He'd been barely breathing by the time he reached the emergency vet's office. Surgery and a blood transfusion had saved his life. It'd been touch-and-go for several days, but then Connor turned a corner. He would have another scar to add to his roster but, otherwise, would make a full recovery.

Jason's phone beeped. He pulled it from his pocket and grinned. "Nathan wants chocolate silk pie from Nelson's Diner."

Addison chuckled. "Tell him you saved his life by fashioning a makeshift tourniquet, and we aren't obligated to bring him desserts every day."

Jason laughed, knowing Addison didn't mean a word of it. When she wasn't taking care of Connor, she was at the Stewart ranch, doing everything possible to make Nathan's recovery easier. The trooper that'd been guarding her house was Addison's third stop. He would also make a full recovery.

Michael and Trevor were in jail. Trevor took a plea bargain and agreed to testify against Michael in exchange for life in prison. Michael kept claiming his innocence, despite a pile of evidence to the contrary. A trial date hadn't been set, but the prosecutor was pushing for a quick one.

Police Chief Walters kept his job—he hadn't known about Trevor's or Michael's involvement—but his political aspirations were over. The scandal would follow him for the rest of his career.

Chloe had gotten her divorce. She'd moved to a new

home close to her mother, and was contemplating her next steps. Becoming a millionaire overnight had opened opportunities. But Chloe was determined to do the very best for her daughter. She was taking things slow.

Jason's phone beeped again, bringing his attention back to the screen. He shook his head. "You've created a monster. Nathan wants me to bring you back to town early enough to watch the last Superman movie."

"Okay, well, I did promise to do that."

"Too bad. He can watch it with you tomorrow." Jason shot off a text to his friend and then tucked his phone back into his pocket. He squeezed Addison's hand. "Ready to see the inside of the cabin?"

She smiled, her eyes sparkling. "Absolutely."

He led the way up the worn steps. The wooden door was weathered. It creaked on the hinges as it swung open, revealing the interior of the cabin.

Addison's eyes widened. "It's lovely."

Jason's heart swelled. His grandfather had built the cabin with his own two hands. It was simple but lovingly made. Outside of family, only a handful of people had ever been here.

He'd wanted Addison to see it. There was something he needed to tell her, and the cabin was a fitting place.

She stepped over the threshold. An old-fashioned wooden stove sat in the center of the tiny living room. Cabinets, burdened by knickknacks like fishing lures and four-leaf clovers, lined one wall. Several paintings in various stages of completion were scattered around the cabin. Dust motes danced in the light streaming through the windows.

Addison ran a hand over the handmade kitchen table. She paused at the pile of sketchbooks on one end. "Are these yours?"

"Yes."

She glanced at him. "May I?"

He nodded, a lump forming in his throat. Addison opened the first sketchbook and flipped through the dark images. Fire. Crumpled and broken bodies. Every ounce of Jason's heartbreak poured onto the page through his pencil.

She stopped at the last page. It was of three men, laughing and smiling. It was the kind of image normally captured by a camera, but he hadn't drawn it from a photograph. The snapshot was embedded in Jason's mind. The last day they were all together. The last moment they were happy.

"Your work..." Addison breathed out. "It's stunning, Jason."

"Even the dark ones?"

She nodded. "All of us have pain. It doesn't mean we're broken, just that we're hurting."

Jason drifted toward the window. Pine trees, ancient but ever-changing, stood sentry. Something inside Jason cracked, the last tether of his resistance. It was time to fulfill the promise he'd made to himself and God.

"Since the bombing, grief has held me in place. It didn't feel right to be happy...to move on." He turned to face her. "Then you burst into my life and everything changed. I love you, Addy. More than I can find words to say how much. I've loved you from the moment we first kissed and probably even before that, but I was too stubborn to realize it. Committed to hurting myself for surviving a bombing that killed my friends."

Tears flooded her eyes. She blinked rapidly, as if to hold them back. "You love me?"

"I love you. And I'm ready to let go of the hurt, Addy.

I'm ready to live my life." He paused. "I hope it'll be with you. We haven't discussed—"

"Stop talking, Jason." She crossed the room. "I love you too."

Jason pulled her into his arms. Their mouths met in a passionate kiss that nearly stopped his heart. He pulled back and traced the curve of her cheek. His future was in her eyes. Marriage. Children. Grandchildren. It took his breath away.

"You were right, Addy. God brought us together for a reason."

She smiled. "Yes, my love. He did." Addison stepped back, trailing a hand down his arm and capturing his hand. She tugged him over to the table. The sketchbook was still open to the drawing of his friends.

Addison touched it. "Will you tell me about them? I want to know everything."

"Yes." Emotion stole his voice, and it took several heartbeats before Jason could trust himself to speak. He brushed a kiss across Addison's temple. "Should we start with the boot camp disaster? Or the time Marcus set a raccoon loose in the commissary?"

ALSO BY LYNN SHANNON

Texas Ranger Heroes Series

Ranger Protection

Ranger Redemption

Ranger Courage

Ranger Faith

Ranger Honor

Triumph Over Adversity Series

Calculated Risk

Critical Error

Covert Action

———

Would you like to know when my next book is released? Or when my novels go on sale? It's easy. Subscribe to my newsletter at www.lynnshannon.com and all of the info will come straight to your inbox!

———

Reviews help readers find books. Please consider leaving a review at your favorite place of purchase or anywhere you discover new books. Thank you.